Musical G
Tongues i̶n̶ ̶A̶s̶p̶i̶c̶ ̶b̶y̶
King Crimson

by Andrew Keeling

Edited by Mark Graham
A Spaceward Publication

Published by Spaceward, Cambridge, UK
ISBN 978-0-9562977-2-3

FIRST EDITION XI, MMX

blurb.com

Please note that musical examples and diagrams referred to in the text fall at the end of each chapter.

Foreword by David Cross

I have just scanned through a copy of Andrew Keeling's Musical Guide to Larks' Tongues in Aspic by King Crimson. In this book Andrew has applied some powerful analytical tools, deconstructing tonal and metrical materials using Bartok's Axis system of tonality, the Golden Section and the Fibonacci series. He has also engaged with the ritualistic, occult and mystical components implicit in the album through the lens of Jungian psychology and revealed some fascinating numerical symbolism (particularly around the number 5) whilst developing a finely argued view of the music's place in the spectrum of rock. Andrew recognises the developmental importance of Larks' Tongues In Aspic in uniting disparate musical features within a shared language as opposed to the polystylism of earlier progressive rock.

This book is rewarding on a number of levels because Andrew is himself an inspiring musician engaging with music he loves. He is eager to listen to the music from any perspective and rules nothing out of his interpretation. The result is a distinctively personal, affectionate but utterly convincing musical analysis and it is a ground-breaking piece of musicology.

Preface

In the Spring of 1972 I returned penniless from touring Ireland in a band. One of the first things to be done on arrival was to phone a friend, and fellow King Crimson-enthusiast, to ask if he'd bought the new post-Islands album, which I'd been reading about and eagerly anticipating. This was Larks' Tongues in Aspic. At that time I couldn't afford to buy a copy myself. An hour later he'd arrived at my house, placed record on turntable and we listened to the album from start to finish. I remember commenting how different I thought the music was. It was surprising. Musically, there'd been considerable change. Things seemed harder-edged, and the saxophones were gone now replaced by violin. Next I looked at the artwork which was somehow 'less' compared to earlier King Crimson albums. I also discovered later, when I'd bought the album myself, there'd been reduction in the lyrical dimension. Those were my first impressions. It took me till 2001/02 to fully understand the musical dimensions of the album and write about those discoveries, although I must stress once again that I'm not a writer. Merely an enthusiast.

Writing at a time when funding for British Universities is under severe threat from a Government who appear confused over the real purpose of education (educare), I make no apologies that concepts in this book might seem, at times, somewhat complex and, even, pedantic. However, it is my view that the music of Larks' Tongues In Aspic demands serious attention, hence the approach used here.

I'd like to thank: Mark Graham and Spaceward for putting time and energy into the project; Robert Fripp for inviting me to write about it in the first place, and for allowing me to reproduce the musical examples; David Cross for enlightening me about King Crimson Mk III; John Wetton for answering my questions about King Crimson Mk III; Sid Smith for his book, In the Court of King Crimson - an invaluable source of information about things Crimson; Hugh O'Donnell of the Discipline Global Mobile art department for the photographs; Jason Walsh for making my original pencil score of Larks' Tongues In Aspic Pt. 2 thoroughly presentable.

Andrew Keeling - February, 2010.

King Crimson
From left to right: Jamie Muir, Bill Bruford, Robert Fripp, David Cross,
John Wetton.

Part 1

1. Larks' Tongues In Aspic (1973) - Mapping the Album

It had been nearly two years since the release of King Crimson's previous studio album, Islands, and Robert Fripp was now the sole surviving member from the original line-up of the band. The genesis of Larks' Tongues In Aspic, the fifth studio album, owes much to Fripp's disillusionment with the first two incarnations of King Crimson, after feeling that the grandiose inclinations of classical Progressive rock were dead, and that the new King Crimson should be a leaner, yet stronger enterprise. (1)

Larks' Tongues In Aspic is the result of the interaction between Fripp and the new members he had recently recruited: Bill Bruford (drums) from the highly successful Yes; John Wetton (bass guitar/vocals) formerly of Mogul Thrash and Family; David Cross, a classical violinist, flautist and keyboardist who was also a composer; Jamie Muir (percussion) from the enclaves of avant-garde jazz. This highly eclectic unit, minus Muir, would be responsible for a further two studio albums, Starless and Bible Black (1973) and Red (1974). The inclusion of Muir looks forward to Pat Mastelotto's contribution on the later Thrak (1995), as well as owing something to former drummer Michael Giles's work on McDonald and Giles's eponymous album (1970). Richard Palmer-

James, a friend of John Wetton's, was also drafted as a lyricist for the three albums, but unlike Peter Sinfield was not to be involved as sleeve-designer, producer or sound-engineer.

With a front-line of Cross and Fripp providing height, line and harmony, and a rhythm section of Wetton and Bruford providing depth, fire-power and incredible rhythmic precision, together with Muir spraying timbral-rhythmic decoration over and within the texture, the stage was set.

The band included the potential for complex polyrhythmic interplay, and the "opposites" which, as we shall discover, are involved in the aural and visual dimensions of the album's architecture appear in the immense range of possibilities provided by the instrumentation. The first incarnation of King Crimson came to prominence through a fusion of musical, philosophical and psychological opposites borne through the interaction of its members. Similar tensions continued to drive this version of the group, as well as being a testing ground for Fripp now unsupported by the original personnel. Gone is the Gothic grandeur of In The Court Of The Crimson King and the poetic quality of the Sinfield-dominated Islands. Instead, the Larks' Tongues incarnation has a more abrasive raw rock approach, particularly during sections of improvisation. It is also a musical unit which allows Fripp's refined guitar and compositional techniques to shine, aligned more with stringed instruments rather than the winds of the Mk I and II versions of the group. Musical residues remain from the original King Crimson in the dimensions of sonority and texture, but on the suface there is less interest in jazz, particularly bearing in mind the absence of saxophones.

Clearly, Larks' Tongues In Aspic betrays the creative rift which had been developing between Fripp and Sinfield prior to and during the making of Islands in late 1971. The more musically extroverted Fripp is heard clearly on the new work, whereas Sinfield's introverted style is represented by his single solo album, Still (1973). Letters written to the music press at the time held the view that Sinfield's album was the true representative of King Crimson, although Fripp insisted that the group had taken on a reality greater and beyond that of the individual members. He came to regard even himself as 'merely a coincidence in Crimson's development' (2), and has added that: 'It is a fundamental mistake for the musician/composer to believe that they are responsible for the music entering the world: they are a necessary condition, not the reason. The sheer willingness and wishing-to-be-heard of music creates a demand which calls on some to give it voice and some to give it ears. How to explain this in terms of Crimson, with its fluctuating membership and several definitive editions? For me, Crimson is a particular individuality which stands apart from the particular group which speak in Crimson's voice. This is the "good fairy" which is not located in any particular band person(s), but which may act through any of them'. (3)

C.G. Jung has called this 'otherness' - which Fripp refers to as King Crimson's 'good fairy' - an archetype and is important in the context of the present discussion. Some commentators have observed that Larks' Tongues In Aspic is a document of an outfit way ahead of its time as well as saying that the record still packs a powerful punch. (4) Why is it that the album remains a groundbreaking work, surpassing many of its contemporaries? I believe there are several different 'voices' on the album: not just instrumental voices, but metaphorical and symbolic voices as well. I will apply different readings to the album which centre around primal, essential and procreative energies as expressed through the music, which have subsequently been expressed by Fripp himself.

1) The primal/ritual voice.
2) Textural accumulation - the sexual voice;
3) The voice of nature;
4) Landscape: the voice of folksong;
5) Structural voices and the hidden world of number.

The discussion will be concluded with analyses of the two framing instrumental pieces, Larks' Tongues In Aspic, Parts 1 and 2, and a music score of the final piece, Larks' Tongues In Aspic Pt 2 is included for reference. During this section of the Musical Guide I have tried to convey the many dimensions of esoterica which appear to underpin LTIA. The most remarkable thing that occurs to me is that LTIA can be read along these lines and, further, the various traditions I have discussed are interconnected by a kind of universal sympathy or correspondence. For King Crimson to have accessed this dimension only helps to reaffirm the band's unique achievement.

2. The Early 1970's

The departure of Peter Sinfield and the new King Crimson line-up coincided with intense upheavals in society at large. The early 1970's brought huge shifts in the political and social orders following the optimism of the 1960 which were, in turn, reflected by the popular arts.

The appearance of Roxy Music in 1972, whose first album was produced by Peter Sinfield, had signified the initial growth of new British art-rock influenced by Lou Reed and the Velvet Underground, The New York Dolls and the New York scene. It was to find its first major British devotee in David Bowie. The impact of the American experimental school had also filtered down to British musicians through the art-schools. The ethos found a footing in the work of improvisers such as Derek Bailey, Gavin Bryars, Tony Oxley and composers Cornelius Cardew, Michael Nyman and Robert Ashley. A direct line can also be traced back to the American avant-garde composers such as Edgard Varese, John Cage and Morton Feldman and, ultimately, to the inspiration of the French artist Marcel Duchamp. Brian Eno's music, post-Roxy Music – in particular his ambient works – are also part of this lineage. Fripp was to collaborate with Eno on the innovative No Pussyfooting album released by Island Records in 1973.

The counter-cultural dream now suddenly seemed defunct. What had started as an anti-establishment reaction and a much-hoped for kick against the US-dominated corporate liberal system had, in the long run, failed to bring about the changes originally hoped for. This now had to be sought in more radical ways. Decadence, and this is what much of the Glam art-rock movement surely was, signified the way forward eventually finding its full-flowering in Punk and the New Wave.

The miner's strikes and the rise of the Trade Unions in Great Britain, coupled with intense anti-Tory feeling and the troubles in Northern Ireland, formed the immediate backdrop to the recording of King Crimson's fifth studio album in the spring of 1972. These were troubled times and felt by many to be a reaction to the golden days of the 1960's.

Initially considered as the epitome of Progressive, it took another two years of King Crimson to engage with the proto-punk ethos eventually found on their seventh studio album, Red, and a further six years for Fripp to fully embrace the New York New Wave stance of Exposure (1978), eventually leading to The League of Gentleman and, finally, King Crimson's Discipline (1981). However, to label King Crimson as Progressive, New Wave or Metal is to miss the point. Instead, King Crimson define, transcend and negate all these styles through an incomparable ability to straddle musical opposites: to be one thing one moment, and something else in another. Perhaps this is what Robert Fripp means when he says that 'Crimson is a way of doing things.' Undoubtedly, tasteful re-invention has been a constant feature of Fripp's approach to King Crimson.

3. Interview with David Cross

So as to contextualise the present writing, I have included an interview with violinist David Cross, who played in King Crimson from 1972 to 1974. I spoke with him about his experiences in King Crimson on the journeys to and from a Cross and Keeling concert at Buckinghamshire New University in September, 2009.

A.K. - How did your association with King Crimson begin?

D.C. – I was in a band that was rehearsing in George's Café on the Fulham Palace Road and Crimson had previously rehearsed there. We were trying to get a record deal and EG Management came down to hear us play, and they brought Robert Fripp with them. Later on, Robert got in touch to say he was getting together with Jamie Muir to record an album of music structured like Indian classical music and asked if I'd like to be involved. I said yes. We went to Jamie's house in Highbury and did some jamming. Robert had an acoustic guitar and I had an acoustic violin. Jamie had a whole floor of percussion instruments. It all seemed quite a good idea and then Robert called me again around the time that Earthbound was being put together. This must have been after the previous Crimson break-up. He said he wanted to try something with Jamie and Bill Bruford of Yes and John Wetton of Family. So we turned up at a rehearsal room in Covent Garden. The five of us just jammed. The theme from Exiles emerged from that first session. It all happened very fast, more or less in one afternoon. It was all very exciting and new for me – I had never seen Yes or Family 'live'. Yes had a reputation for being very skilled performers and creating intricate compositions and Family had 'englishness'. I knew nothing much about King Crimson. The music seemed to shape-up well and there was a lot of energy about. Bill was still in Yes and had to make a decision whether to leave them the same afternoon. Also, did we continue with the name King Crimson or move on and do something new? Bill decided it was time for a career change and the new King Crimson was born. A press photographer turned up and the photo of us all appeared on the front page of Melody Maker two days later. I was that close to not doing it. My grandfather's funeral was on the same day as the Covent Garden session. I always felt some guilt about missing the funeral, although my family was always OK about it.

The 1972 version of King Crimson was a cut-off: making a point to be in the real world and a conscious decision to be unlike the first King Crimson. In the Court of the Crimson King had to go, but the king had to go on. There was a definite line/shift between the earlier King Crimson and the band I was in. There was a contemporaneity to the band and a broader frame of references. The Jamie Muir version of the band raised the bar quite a bit in terms of the range of possibilities.

The head, heart and hips analysis was Robert's idea for balanced music. There was a lot of male gesturing and we got fed up when there were mostly men in the audience at some gigs. I found it disturbing. I felt something was wrong when the music was appealing to a small percentage of the population. Why was this? Male rock gesturing targeted women, but it was only men who appreciated it.

A.K - Were you aware of The Mahavishnu Orchestra?

D.C. - I had no interest in harmonic jazz, probably as a reaction to my father's generation. I was into modal jazz like Coltrane but not really into Be-bop. I didn't get the Mahavishnu Orchestra although John and Bill were well aware of them. Robert never mentioned it. On The Inner Mounting Flame there's a sense of ascension with keys moving up in 3rds and so on. Robert never suggested that I 'listen to this.' Rather, I was into late Beethoven String Quartets, Bartok and Stravinsky. My interest in odd metres came from an interest in Bartok's string quartets. I'd always seen 3+3+2 rhythms, for instance, as quaver-based units like a succession of differently metered bars. That I'd begun to see them as syncopation came mainly through discussion and playing with Bill Bruford. Robert and I were on the same wavelength in many ways, and I understood musically a lot of what he was doing. It was a nice balance between Robert and I. We got on well and tried to work out the lead lines. It was obvious that Bill and John got together and talked about rhythm. I never had a problem contextualising what Robert meant and did.

A.K. – Can you say more about the differences and similarities between the first version of the band and yours?

D.C. – Robert felt there was a Crimson way of doing things, yet I didn't feel the continuity in terms of principles and aims. I'm talking about the first Crimson and my version of the band. The mellotron was a linking factor between them. I met Mel Collins recently and I'm sure he was insulted with what I said that early Crimson sounded like bad film music. I think it took me a while to appreciate some of the more interesting qualities of the mellotron – a bit like using black and white footage in a 'Technicolor' movie.

The other thing that could have linked them was the opening-up to different styles. The first Crimson was an act of rock/jazz/folk/classical fusion whereas we were writing in the 'now' when the fusion had already occurred. Robert said that he didn't want Michael Giles to play with cymbals but rather to play with drums. I read this as a connection to timpani in orchestras and cymbals as a jazz reference. The music was put together differently. Bill and John had a drive for rhythmic exploration. Robert and I had an understanding of the melodic materials but there was also a lot of holistic musicianship going on and Bill particularly listened intently to everything. There were options there. We were much more part of the twentieth century. The first Crimson referred back to nineteenth century Romantic music. If there was a Crimson way of doing things it involved a degree of musical competence and aural ability along with a receptivity – being open to everything. Robert was probably selective all the time but he never raised barriers.

A.K. – Was Larks' Tongues brought into being primarily through Robert Fripp, or was there a 'band mind' at work?

D.C. – Robert Fripp's view of the world was not opposed to the scene at that time. Primitivism was part of bands like Principal Edwards Magic Theatre, and was an important thread in rock. Everyone was aware of Stravinsky, and not just Robert. He picked people he could work with and encouraged them to grow, creatively speaking, and as people too. He presented himself as a performer and composer, and the music emerged as a collision of experience. Wetton and Bruford were steamingly creative. There were a couple of methodologies at work: first, jamming – particularly Jamie's view of being in the moment and letting things happen; secondly, composition and song-writing. Robert brought things that were written. I brought things but I wasn't confident in presenting ideas at that time. There were great compositions from Robert, but they were given life by the other people in the band. The attitude of the other people can either block or enrich the emerging material. We were all creators who brought something different to the table but we were also facilitators willing to smooth the path for each other. There was a fantastic fusion of improvisation and composition in that King Crimson. A lot of the more beautiful lines are down to John Wetton. He was particularly inventive and is a great musical romantic. His vocal lines demonstrate this. King Crimson was a coincidence of perspectives. This view takes nothing away from Robert who allowed the music to grow quite naturally. He didn't push and dominate but he did respond musically to what was going on and I guess the worst thing for any of us was when the others didn't respond!

4. Interview with John Wetton

A.K. - What was the writing process in King Crimson? How exactly did it work? (i.e. how democratic was the band?)

J.W. - Democratic. Robert would have formally written pieces, but group compositions could come from anywhere. People have a misconception about rehearsal/writing protocol: there were no rules, and cross-fertilization came from all sides. I mooted 'Starless' for instance a full year before we started work on it, because nobody bit on it first time around. I had presented it at the wrong time. When it was married with Robert's/David's intro and Bill's demonic bass riff, it was born.

A.K. - Did you work out songs (musical ideas) with Richard Palmer James?

J.W. - No. Richard would receive a track, with my la-dum-dum vocal guide for syllables, 'starless' alternatives. I saw The Night Watch text and fell in love with it. When a Fripp melody came up which matched the lyric, I suggested a marriage, and got a credit for that function. All I did was crowbar and hammer the whole thing together, but it was deemed enough of a contribution to merit my name going on it. Lament also existed before we got hold of it, but it was my melody on that one. As with most bands, there were many different ways to skin a cat, but whenever you hear vocal and bass in parallel harmony (Easy Money), that's usually me. I've been squarely criticized (inside and outside the band) for One More Red Nightmare, but I've been delighted that both times I've done Philadelphia School of Rock, that song is the clear, runaway favorite for the kids to perform. They love everything about it, including the song/lyrics.

A.K. - Essentially, did Robert Fripp allow you full control over the melodic detail in the songwriting? I ask because LTIA, coming after KC Mk II (the 'off the road' and then, Boz-Mel-Ian version on the band), marks a dividing line in KC musical output. i.e. stylistically a distinct break from the MK I and Mk II versions of the band, as far as I can tell.

J.W. - The LTIA band couldn't have been more different from the previous incarnation. We were all pulling in the same direction most of the time, and melodic detail was discussed, not dogmatized.

A.K. - There's an unreleased track from the Red days called Blue. Would this have appeared on the album following Red if the band had continued?

J.W. - I'd like to think so. It was/is a ballsachingly beautiful piece.

A.K. - Did you ever write with Ian McDonald? I know he was about to re-join post-Red.

J.W. - I've written with Ian for his solo album Drivers Eyes, and for my solo album Welcome to Heaven. We remain firm friends, and I'd have been delighted if the band had continued with him in '74.

A.K. - How intensive were rehearsals in the early days of KC Mk III? I know you played in Family (I saw you with them in Blackpool, btw). How different was KC to a band like Family?

J.W. - Family was a great way for me to find the stage without suffering the spotlight, in KC the spotlight was shared, as were all other duties. There was the same light and shade in both bands, both could be gentle, yielding one minute, and cataclysmic testosterone the next, but that's quintessential English rock,isn't it?

A.K. - I know you've played with a wide spectrum of the 'great' bands from the 1970's. Can you say which one stands at the top of the list?

J.W. - No. I moved around in the mid '70s out of necessity. Roxy was great fun, Heep taught me about loyalty, but I wish Crimson could have lasted a bit longer with me in it. That wasn't to be, but there was no-one better at doing what they did than the individuals in that band.

A.K. - How did you add bass parts to RF's musical ideas? How did he add guitar parts to your's and David's ideas?

J.W. - It was just instinctive most of the time, you don't decide to play with a fellow because he is so good, then chuck his ideas out with the teabags.

A.K. - How much of KC Mk III's music came from improvisation?

J.W. - Quite a bit, around 50/50 on a good night, but on that good night the improvisation was so good that the audience really couldn't tell which was formal and what was improvisation. Just at the point where the fantasy was either going to a) climax, or b) fall apart, we could invoke a rocker, or a ballad which would firmly remind the audience that we were there.

5. The Primal/Ritual Voice

The fact that Larks' Tongues In Aspic includes content based on ancient ritual, as well as structural, motivic and rhythmic unity, points to the possibility that it follows a modernist paradigm. This is connected to the musical influences of the members of King Crimson Mk III at the time (Stravinsky and Bartók and, to some extent, The Mahavishnu Orchestra), whereas Peter Sinfield's Still, a close contemporary of LTIA, as I shall refer to it, is more concerned with different stylistic juxtapositions which give it more of a postmodern stance.

What precisely are the narrative concerns of LTIA? The undercoding means that listeners receive an almost unconscious, somewhat vague, yet mysterious sense of meaning when experiencing the music. However, Book Of Saturday, the second song on the album is, according to King Crimson's biographer Sid Smith, '...about sex' connecting it to the ritualistic concerns I have so far discussed. The third song, Exiles, is an elegy for a lost England: to be specific, Richard Palmer-James's emotional outpouring about his homeland during an enforced stay in Europe in the early 1970's. There are further connections between Book Of Saturday and the fourth song, Easy Money, in terms of 'the game' (prostitution and sex) which casts a backward glance to earlier King Crimson repertoire such as Cadence And Cascade from In The Wake Of Poseidon, and Ladies Of The Road from Islands.

More specifically, Robert Fripp has said that he had always been impressed by Stravinsky's The Rite Of Spring (1913). 'If you were to ask my aim...it was to access the energy and power of Hendrix...but to expand the vocabulary... notably via Bartók...and the early Stravinsky of the Firebird and The Rite Of Spring' (5). In this way it might be possible to read LTIA as a kind of musical 'rite' - a ritual - where the primal instincts of both performers and listeners are brought into play. These kinds of instincts are, of course, at the root of ancient rituals which The Rite Of Spring symbolises. J.G. Frazer's epic anthropological epic, The Golden Bough, includes a section on sympathetic magic, detailing such primordial customs as vegetation rites.

In ancient times real people represented deities not simply as an allegory, but intending to bring about Spring growth by a kind of sympathetic magic. In other words, the marriage of trees and plants could not be made fertile without the real mirror of the human act of procreation (6). Fripp has written that LTIA Part 2, '...accesses the same stream of primal, procreative energies as The Rite Of Spring. LTIA Part 2 is a description of the sexual act - from one point of view. A "rite of spring" which was well recognised by the producers of the film Emmanuelle' (7). The album may be compared to a primal, or primordial rite which is underlined musically by the use of traditional instruments such as kalimba and talking drum juxtaposed with music of great rhythmic barbarity performed on 'electric' instruments.

The huge textural accumulations and climaxes may be read as metaphors for sexual arousal and orgasm. LTIA bears similar characteristics to D.H. Lawrence's The Plumed Serpent, T.S. Eliot's The Waste Land, the ballets of Diaghilev, Roerich and Stravinsky and the work of Picasso which all have primitivism at their centres. In this way LTIA engages the listener in a kind of musico-psychological ritual, awakening the psyche at the level of the collective unconscious.

Comparisons between certain aspects of the Stravinsky and the King Crimson works opens-up a complex discussion which cannot be fully dealt with here. However, the overall structural shaping of the works may be broadly termed 'ritualistic', and includes tableaux-like blocks, octatonic and modal pitch materials and folksong. The overt sexuality of the album is intensified by the inclusion of instruments associated with rock music in much the same way as in the music of Jimi Hendrix, but clearly the band realised that a different type of musical expression was required for the album, and one that might be centred more on ritualistic concerns.

LTIA might also be regarded as an expression of the Mortificatio episode in the Alchemical Opus, where darkness, depression and death - and symbols associated with it such as dismemberment, mutilation, suffering, slaying, sacrifice, exile and so on - are a necessary prelude for rebirth. This is a particularly potent metaphor for LTIA as a whole, and also for King Crimson who, at that time, were in the process of reformation and transformation from Mk I/II (1969 and 1970/71 respectively) into the Mk III version. I will develop this aspect of LTIA later.

6. Textural Accumulation - The Sexual Voice of Larks' Tongues In Aspic

LTIA plunges a listener into a sound-world of extreme light and shade, combined with tremendous surges in the music's foward-motion. These structural spans create tension arriving at overpowering musical climaxes. The beginning of LTIA Part 1 is a case in point. Following the delicacy of the soft gamelan-like introduction which includes kalimba, thumb-piano, looped violin, glockenspiel and multi-tracked bells, a 10/8 rhythm appears in the solo violin, at timing-counter number 2:54, which is episodic in character. This triggers a gradual textural accumulation directed at the point of arrival (3:40): an immense hammer-blow of charged, distorted electric guitar plus the full band ensemble of bass, drums and percussion. This kind of growth in textural density also occurs during the instrumental episodes of Easy Money, The Talking Drum (the fifth piece) and the ascending, sustained lyrical music heard during LTIA Part 2. Once a climax has been achieved the music plunges back into the depths where the directional up and thrust begins again.

The Talking Drum is one huge accumulation of textural and dynamic intensity leading to the final screaming climax at 7:19, which anticipates the vigorous, rhythmic drive of LTIA Part 2.

This represents the sexual union of male and female in a kind of musical heirosgamos, or sacred marriage. Structurally, it is the ultimate point of arrival in the work. Instrumental lines often ascend which, when underpinned by the rhythm section, reinforce the idea of orgasm and climax. It is also reminiscent of the shaping of lines previously used by Fripp during the guitar solo of Ladies Of The Road from Islands, which also depicts orgasm. However, in the case of LTIA there is great intensification of means towards the representation of the sexual act. Accumulating densities such as these are also found in The Rite Of Spring, particularly during the introduction of the section L'Adoration de le Terre with its its dramatic cut-off just before figure 12 (see The Rite Of Spring. Boosey and Hawkes study score, page 8).

7. The Voice of Nature

When probed about the meaning of the title at the time of the album's release in the Spring of 1973, Robert Fripp replied, '... along the lines of "something precious trapped in matter" ' (8). The phrase has far-reaching implications from which we are able to reach some kind of understanding through the term 'nature'.

What is meant by 'nature' in this context? Fripp had become interested in the occult through a friend, Walli Elmlark, which gives his phrase a personal as well as a metaphorical ring. Both Fripp and David Cross admired the music of Bela Bartók which includes techniques based on natural phenomena such as the Golden Section, which I will discuss later. It seems to me that these two ideas are both sides of the same coin deriving from the natural order, which mirror the inner workings of the cosmos. The occultist, like the artist, is able to manipulate materials by bringing to pass hidden, yet dynamic transformations in the environment. Cosmology is a way of perceiving the natural order, by involving many diverse and esoteric disciplines. During the mid-1970's Fripp developed his cosmological interests in relation to the work of J.G. Bennett. Fripp has said: 'If any writing is to be "true" then its form will appear to be based on cosmological principles (i.e. Golden Section) in terms of structure and, possibly, pitches. It will be inevitable rather than intentional - this may be both involutionary and evolutionary' (9). That LTIA is couched in secrecy is part of both the mysterious attraction of the album and, at the same time, part of the esoteric nature of occult disciplines. This factor lies at the heart of the work.

Symbols such as those that stand for the gestation and birth of the creative impulse in such ancient traditions as Gnosticism or Alchemy might also serve as suitable metaphors for Fripp's definition of the title of the work. In bringing to birth something precious from matter - a kind of musical Philosophers' Stone - through the natural order as represented in music, a listener encounters a kind of musical/magical 'filius philosophorum' shot-through with musical opposites, which is part of the mysterious psycho-physical make-up of the Philosphers' Stone. The Alchemical Opus was empowered by the hermaphroditic spirit Hermes-Mercurius who stood as a symbol for the opposites contained in the Stone. There are also parallels here with Fripp's comment that the music of King Crimson is influenced by the 'good-fairy' aspect (see Andrew Keeling - Musical Guide to In The Court of the Crimson King p. 126 for a fuller discussion). The cosmological concerns I have mentioned are also connected with Jung's psychology where the creative impulse is often thought of as being archetypal in origin. In this way it might be possible to posit the idea that 'nature' is to be found in LTIA at an organic level.

a) 'Good fairy' = creative impulse = archetype = phenomenon of nature = Hermes-Mercurius =

b) Masculine/feminine, Sol et Luna (Alchemical symbolism), animus/anima (Jungian terminoloy), rational/intuitive = Fripp/Elmlark = sexual metaphor = alchemical coniunctio =

c) Birth of the 'filius philosophorum' (Philosophers' Stone) = LTIA =

d) Golden Section forms = octatony/folksong/pentatony.

8. Landscape - the Voice of Folksong and Modes

a) The English Voice

LTIA gives voice to 'Englishness', but an 'englishness' which is a long way removed from the poetic rhetoric of some other progressive rock of the period. Each member of King Crimson Mk III brought this particular characteristic to the music. Robert Fripp has said: 'My own Englishness is never far away for example, in Book Of Saturday and Pie Jesu (a later Soundscape piece) but in Larks' my Englishness drifts towards the continent' (10).

A recorded King Crimson performance from the period (17-10-73 - the Bremen Beat Club. DGM Collectors' Club No. 3, Februrary 1999) finds the group singing with quite a different voice from that of its close contemporaries. There is a greater sense of angularity and irregularity, not to mention intensity, in terms of line and rhythm superficially recalling, in part, The Mahivishnu Orchestra. However, in LTIA Part 1 it is possible to recognise some music that also has some affinity with Vaughan Williams' work, particularly The Lark Ascending. In LTIA a connection can be made with English modality, but a modal language juxtaposed with another modal language sounding as though there might be a European source present.

The Lark Ascending, which is referred to in the context of LTIA Part 1, is called a Romance. It is also a Rhapsody which is a particularly English musical form. Vaughan Williams's A Norfolk Rhapsody and Holst's Egdon Heath are other prime examples of the genre, and connected to the idea of a landscape peculiar to England: gently rolling pastures, partitioned by stone walls and intersected by the many rivers that wind their way through the rural landscape, sometimes including dramatic features such as crags, moorland and mountains. The Lark Ascending is a metaphorical landscape piece complete with arching and soaring lines in the solo violin part held secure within an unfolding form, complete with cadenza-like passages reminiscent of flight and birdsong. LTIA Part 1 falls within this category and may also be likened to Fripp's more recent Soundscape pieces. Some of these have a certain resonance with the landscape metaphor through the layering of lines in creating large-scale contrapuntal textures, in turn bringing about perspectives of foreground and background. Cross' violin texture in LTIA undoubtedly connects LTIA to the English Pastoral tradition, just as Jerry Goodman's violin connects The Mahavishnu Orchestra to the Celtic tradition.

Some of LTIA is modal, along with musics derived from folksong sources. Modes allow for rolling, often repeated and sectionalised forms which, because of the weakened and, even, absent strong Dominant key, in turn create weak points of arrival. Rather, climaxes are achieved by dramatic textural accumulations or increases in tempi, rather than by harmonic impetus. Tableaux-like stuctures are something of a trademark for early and mid-twentieth century New English Renaissance composers, and the music, shot-through with folksong material - either real or close quotations - became an important musical fingerprint for English nationalism. Folk musics also have implications for organic unity within large-scale structures. For example, how is it possible for a composer to treat a folksong? The possibilities are that it can either be played once and then repeated more loudly; welded into a Sonata form structure (see Vaughan Williams's Pastoral Symphony); treated in a rhapsodic-like way to create tableaux-like works where the effect becomes ritualistic or processional-like with each section partitioned-off from the previous one. LTIA, as well as some of John Tavener's works for example, shares some of these concerns.

The sections of sustained, lyrical music found in LTIA Pt 2 is also reminiscent of some of the motivic material found in the Finale (Rondo Capriccioso) of Vaughan Williams's First String Quartet in G minor, a key work in the composer's oeuvre.

b) The European Voice - Bartók's Axis System of Tonality

The European language, accessed in LTIA along with octatonicism, is Bartók's Axis System of Tonality which David Cross and Robert Fripp seem to have unconsciously utilised. This is a system where new relationships exist between keys. By drawing-up a key-wheel and assigning a place to each key within a circle of fifths, the following relationships emerge. (See Diagrams 1 and 2).

It can be seen that chords of C, A, F# and Eb take on a Tonic (I) function; chords of E, C# (Db), A# (Bb), and G take on a Dominant (V) function; chords of Ab (G#), B, D and F take on a Subdominant (IV) function. Ernö Lendvai, who was responsible for codifying Bartók's system of pitch organisation, makes the point that a harmonic pole corresponds to its counterpole without any change in its function (11). He also states that the system was one steeped in tradition by providing a functionalism excluded in other systems of twentieth century music.

As applied to LTIA, the axis system of keys provides an interesting perspective to some of the harmonic organisation found in it. The axes are presented outside the context of the wheel, and in this case with G as the Tonic which is the pitch/key centre of the work. (See Diagram 3).

For example, the axis system makes a fluid transition in the context of LTIA Part 2, allowing keys to be categorised easily in either Tonic, Dominant or Subdominant roles. The example below demonstrates that I, IV and V are active from 0:00 - 0:29 (bars 1-13), which prepares for the sustained lyrical music at 0:46 (bar 20). This can be spelt as IV/I and, therefore, a modulation by means of the axis occurs. (See Diagram 4).

The riffs, found during the first section of the piece at 0:08, 0:17 and 0:27 (bars 4, 8 and 12) use the interchangeable harmonic poles of I, IV and V. (See Diagram 5).

The system allows the music to modulate to traditionally unrelated keys, but ones which are now axially-related, by sonically supplying the music with both a greater harmonic differentiation and fluidity through its connection to the tonal tradition. In the context of rock this is more fitting than, say, atonality might be. Fripp has said that, 'I don't doubt the centres are axis-based although at the time I wouldn't have been able to articulate it in those terms' (12). As we shall see in using the axis system, which is related to octatonicism, pentatony and the Golden Section, King Crimson are aligning listeners with 'nature' by dipping into 'the pool of information' as Fripp has expressed his cosmological concerns (13).

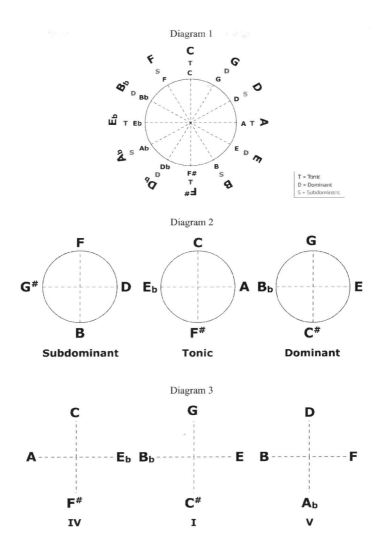

Diagram 1

T = Tonic
D = Dominant
S = Subdominant

Diagram 2

Subdominant   Tonic   Dominant

Diagram 3

IV   I   V

Musical Guide to Larks' Tongues in Aspic by King Crimson

Diagram 4

Bar 1-3(0:00-0:05)	4(0:08)	5(0:10)	8(0:17)	9(0:20)	12(0:27)	13-14(0:29-0:32)	20-21(0:46-0:49)	24(0:57)	28(1:07)	31(1:15)
I	I		IV	V	V	V	IV/I	V/I	V	V

Diagram 5

Bar	4	8	12
	I--->	IV--->	V

40

c) The Golden Section

Some of the positioning of important musical events in LTIA is by the use of the Golden Section. Golden Section is the division of a distance, or duration, so that the proportion of the whole distance to the longer section geometrically correlates to the proportion of the longer to the smaller section. This means that the longer section is the geometric mean of the whole distance and the smaller part. If the whole length is equal to 1, then the value of the longer section is 0.618, while the smaller section is 0.382. (See Diagram 6).

Bartók's structural techniques employ the Golden Section, and many of his works demonstrate the principle (14).For example, the first movement of his Sonata for Two Pianos and Percussion is 433 bars in length, with the recapitulation beginning at bar 274. This is the point of Golden Section (433 x 0.618 = 274).

A similar principle, and one related to Golden Section, is the Fibonacci sequence of numbers. Here, a number is equal to the sum of the ones that precede it. If the whole were considered to be 13, the place of Golden Section (0.618) would be 8. (See Diagram 7).

When a musical event is positioned by employing the Golden Section, a listener is likely to experience a sense of structural 'rightness' about the form. As a composer, Bartók was influenced by nature and thought that folk music, and its formation, developed as spontaneously as natural organisms (15).

The same principle is at work in LTIA Part 1. For example, the first section is unmetered, and performed improvisationally. The whole section is 2'-54" long: a delicate, gamelan-like collage consisting of kalimba (thumb piano), glockenspiel(s), violin and multi-tracked bells which provide the music with an Afro-Indonesian flavour. There is one attack - a 'signal' - from a talking-drum at 1:36 that brings the kalimba to momentary halt. The glockenspiel(s), violin and bells fade in one by one, following the kalimba that initially leads the ensemble. By 2'-48" the violin and glockenspiel(s) have faded leaving the bells alone. 0'-57" is the place where the violin enters. By taking 2'-48" as the overall structural division within the first formal span of the piece, it can be seen that the violin enters at Fibonacci :3 (2.48 x 3 -:- 13 = 0.57). 1'-52" is the point at which all the instruments are dead centre of the sound-space. Afterwards the kalimba moves to the right-hand channel, and there is a gradual fading-out of the violin, glockenspiel and kalimba. 1'-52" is the place of Golden Section, or Fibonnaci :8 (2.48 x 8 -:- 13 = 1.52).

Robert Fripp has written about his interest in Bartók's instinctive compositional processes: 'I didn't and don't have the technical qualifications or capacity to know what was involved. But I did read music and spent my unemployment in London with Stevens's volume "Bartók" while practising guitar. We might recall that the young Stravinsky of The Rite Of Spring didn't "know" what he was doing either: for him it was more on instinctive and intuitive processes. And Bartók described his own compositional processes as instinctive and intuitive. If musical material does emerge instinctively and intuitively, we might postulate that anyone who adopts this approach might be accessing the same "pool of information". Formally, this leads to the arithmetic approach...and the geometric approach (i.e. Bartók and the Golden Section). The first has the characteristic of stability, the second of dynamism. The first is crystalline, the second vital. This applies vertically (pitch, and therefore, melody and harmony) and horizontally (rhythm)' (16). Fibonacci may also be applied to pitch material in terms of interval structure. It is seen in pitches that make up pentatonic collections. (Intervals, here, are counted out in semitones: G=0, G#=1, A=2 etc). (See Example 1).

It also figures in the octatonic scales favoured by Stravinsky, Bartók and King Crimson. (See Example 2).

It is only one further step in seeing that the octatonic scale, as well as being 'double symmetrical' (here, the Plagal octatonic form which alternates tones with semitones; the Authentic octatonic alternates semitones with tones), is connected to the Axis system. (See Example 3).

I will discuss pitch during the analyses of LTIA Parts 1 and 2, but suffice to say there are many examples of octatonic and modal scales (especially 0-2-3-5 tetrachords) found during the work.

It seems that King Crimson used Golden Section principles unconsciously, as well as the modes and scales connected with it. Fripp: 'My approach in choosing a mode is not usually to consult a scale encyclopaedia or lexicon, but to assemble the notes which speak to me. Then to discover what made this might be so that the brain can then get engaged. For example, a new piece, "EleKctriKc" (2001), wasn't meant to be a combination of the whole-tone and symmetrical scales: that's what it is...reading Lendvai, for example, made sense after the event' (17).

The conclusion to be drawn is that the Golden Section and modes are combined within the 'pool of information' that Fripp has mentioned, deriving from the broad cosmological scheme of things. Jonathan Goldman has written: 'According to Hans Kayser (a twentieth century German scientist), the whole number ratios of musical harmonics corresponds to an underlying framework existing in chemistry, crystallography, astronomy, architecture, spectroanalysis, botany and the study of other natural sciences. The relationship expressed in the periodic table of elements, an understanding of the formation of matter, resembles the overtone structure in music.' (18).

Musical Guide to Larks' Tongues in Aspic by King Crimson

Diagram 6

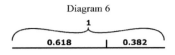

Diagram 7

2, 3, 5, 8, 13, (21, 34, 55, 89)

↑

G.S.

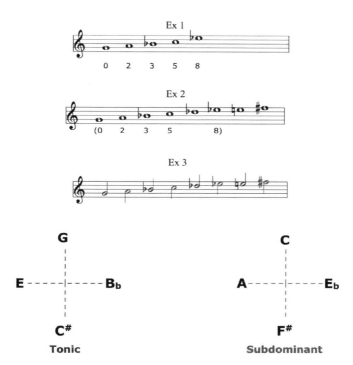

9. Structural Voices

It's my understanding that the structure of LTIA arose from a balance of improvisation and composition. The composer Robin Walker has made the distinction between form and structure in a musical piece (19), and my experience as part of the Cross and Keeling improvisation duo has clarified that improvisation might be termed *organic*, whereas much written composition might be thought of as *synthetic* (20). However, the key to any successful piece is likely to be a combination of both. If the unconscious has a direction of its own, is atemporal and ground in nature, then it follows that unconscious performance (i.e. improvisation) - and, even, unconscious composition - is likely to create its own unique forms which might be termed organic or, at least, archetypal in origin.

Instrumental pieces and songs are equally represented on LTIA:

1) Larks' Tongues In Aspic Part 1 (instrumental)
2) Book Of Saturday (song)
3) Exiles (song)
4) Easy Money (song)
5) Talking Drum (instrumental)

6) Larks' Tongues In Aspic Part 2 (instrumental).

There are similarities in the positioning of the material as compared to previous King Crimson albums (21). (See Diagram 8).

There is also some similarity between textural types:

1) 21st Century Schizoid Man/Pictures Of A City/LTIA Pt 1 - multi-sectional, riff-based, contrasting softer sections;

2) I Talk To The Wind/Cadence And Cascade/Book Of Saturday - reduced textures, sandwiched between two louder pieces;

3) Epitaph/In The Wake Of Poseidon/Exiles - mellotron-based, hymn-like;

4) Moonchild/Catfood/Ladies Of The Road/Easy Money - humorous, novelty song, social comment;

5) In The Court Of The Crimson King/The Devil's Triangle/Song Of The Gulls/Islands/The Talking Drum/LTIA Pt 2 - multi-sectional, climax of work(s).

There is also a clear and similar sense of pacing throughout each album:

       1) Riff-based/strident/fast;
       2) Song with reduced texture/medium tempo/'love' song;
       3) Epic hymn-like song/moderate tempo/philosophical
       4) 'Novelty' song/medium fast in tempo;
       5) Climax/multi-sectional/ostinato-based.

Gregory Karl has found narrative practices common to the first five King Crimson studio albums, in terms of a fictional subject who experiences dangerous trials (22). I would suggest that the perils encountered by the fictional subject of LTIA may be compared to a rite-of-passage: a metaphorical death and re-birth of a sacrificial victim symbolised by the 'death' heard in LTIA Pt 1, and the exuberant round-dance of LTIA Pt 2. This correlates with the death and renewal of the earth in Spring vegetation rites, and is more sophisticated in this context as compared to the counter-cultural statements found on the first four King Crimson albums. It also goes some way in representing the changing fashions within the music industry of the period 1972-73, when the initial creative explosion of progressive rock was in decline.

The two long pieces which frame the structure are LTIA Pt 1 and Pt 2 which are 13'-36" and 7'-03" respectively. Robert Fripp has written: ' Larks' 1 was conceived as the beginning of a King Crimson performance and Larks' 2 as the end. Larks' 1, as a whole, contains more ideas and input from all the team than Larks' 2 which follows more closely my own personal vision' (23). The remaining instrumental piece, The Talking Drum, sits in the penultimate place as a huge anacrusis into LTIA Pt 2. The three songs are placed centrally. There is an enormous range of textural, harmonic and rhythmic contrast, so that each is felt as a point of arrival on the sonic journey.

The character of each instrumental piece and song is tied-up with the mode centre of each. Positioning of song types, within the architecture, seems to be an important concern as on previous King Crimson albums, and here the relationships between parts of the whole are particularly well refined. Diagrams 9 and 10 show that the two instrumental Larks' pieces are related by modal centres on G, and that the A mode connects the beginning of LTIA Pt 1 with Book Of Saturday and The Talking Drum, which mirror each other. (See Diagrams 9 and 10). The A centre is also felt in a quasi-dominant relationship to the D centre of Exiles, as well as to the final point of arrival (D major) in the coda of LTIA Pt 2. An E modal centre connects the end of Exiles and Easy Money. The original vinyl version of the record allows for a break between Exiles, at the end of side 1, picked-up by Easy Money at the beginning of the second side.

Diagram 8

In The Court Of The Crimson King	**In The Wake Of Poseidon**	**Islands**	**Larks' Tongues In Aspic**
1) 21st Century Schizoid Man	= Pictures Of A City	= Formentera Lady	= Larks' Part 1
2) I Talk To The Wind	= Cadence and Cascade	= Sailor's Tale	= Book Of Saturday
3) Epitaph	= In The Wake Of Poseidon	= The Letters	= Exiles
4) Moonchild	= Catfood	= Ladies Of The Road	= Easy Money
5) The Court Of The Crimson King	= The Devil's Triangle	= Song of The Gulls/Islands	= Talking Drum/Larks' Part 2

Diagram 9

	Larks' Pt 1	Book Of Saturday	Exiles	Easy Money	Talking Drum	Larks' Pt 2
a)	13'-36"	2'-49"	7'-40"	7'-45"	7'-26"	7'-03"
b)	Varied texture (instrumental)	Reduced texture (song)	Full texture (song)	Full texture (song)	Varied texture (instrumental)	Varied texture (instrumental)
c)	Violin, guitar, Bass, Drums, various perc.	Vocals, violin, guitar, bass	Vocals, violin, guitar flute, mellotron, piano drums, perc. 'noise', bass	Vocals, guitars, mellotron, bass, drums, perc.	Violin, guitar, bass, drums, perc. 'noise'	Violin, guitars, bass, drums, perc.

Songs

Instrumental pieces

Anacrusis

Diagram 10

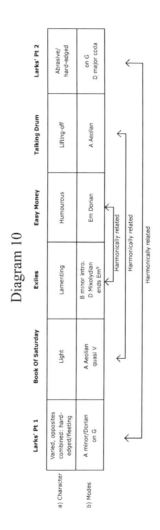

	Larks' Pt 1	Book Of Saturday	Exiles	Easy Money	Talking Drum	Larks' Pt 2
a) Character	Varied, opposites combined: hard-edged/fleeting	Light	Lamenting	Humourous	Lifting-off	Abrasive/hard-edged
b) Modes	A minor/Dorian on G	A Aeolian quasi V	B minor intro. D Mixolydian ends Em^9	Em Dorian	A Aeolian	on G D major coda

Harmonically related

Harmonically related

Harmonically related

10. The Hidden World of Number

There may also be another, perhaps more meaningful structural possibility. If LTIA Pts 1 and 2 are considered as being one and the same piece, each including harmonies, riffs, lines and motives in common to each other, or if The Talking Drum is considered as being connected to LTIA Pt 2, then there are five pieces in all. (See Diagram 11). The number 5 is significant throughout King Crimson's output appearing on In The Court Of The Crimson King and In The Wake Of Poseidon and resurfacing here. Fripp had become interested in cosmology and, especially, occultism (Wicca and related disciplines), which was part of the scene in the early 1970's.

This could mean that, in terms of numerology, the number 5 is an important cosmological/occult signifier working at a musico-archetypal level. Isadore Kazminsky has said that 5 is regarded as having intense vibration as well as its relationship with the Kabbalah where it represents the five letters in the name of God (24). It also means that the pentagram could take on an interesting structural-cosmological signifier, and one which may relate to its role in invocation and banishing.

Five is also the number of 'man'. There were five playing members in this incarnation of King Crimson, each member, perhaps also aligned with one of the five elements of Chinese alchemy (wood, air, fire, earth and water), and LTIA became the fifth album with the deletion of the 'live' Earthbound album. 5 is also regarded as the number of rebirth which this album clearly represents following the demise of the previous groups. Other aspects of 5-ness are pentatonic pitch collections; the interval of the Diminished 5th which was also used by Stravinsky and Rimsky-Korsakov as a musico-supernatural symbol. There are also many examples of 5/4 (10/8) metres to be found. I will elaborate on this aspect during the section on rhythm.

The cover-art of LTIA is specifically Tantric in design. Tantra is the ancient Indian art of inner alchemy. Through esoteric and sexual practices, together with meditation and Kundalini yoga, Tantrists sought to unify the inner microcosmic world of psyche with the outer macrocosm of nature. Sex was considered a ritual of prime spiritual import by uniting male and female elements in the cosmos represented by such symbols as sun and moon, Shiva and Shakti. By channelling energy from the lower parts of the body to the upper through sexual orgasm, inner transformation could be achieved, in much the same way as the Alchemists sought transmutation of materials in their laboratories. The Tantric process is nowhere better encountered in a modern context than in LTIA. It makes its presence felt in many of the musical symbols on the album such as the lark's flight in the central section of the first piece, the accumulative/orgasmic music of both title pieces and The Talking Drum, and the sexual imagery of Book Of Saturday and Easy Money. The ultimate outworking of Fripp's interest in esoteric systems is to be found on his solo album Exposure (1977), which includes the philosophy of J.G. Bennett, and G. I. Gurdjieff, at its epicentre.

This also relates to the cover art of the album, which is Tantric but also Hermetic. The ancient alchemical treatise, The Emerald Tablet, says: '...whatever is below is like that which is above, and whatever is above is like that which is below.... It's father is the sun and its mother is the moon...For this reason I am called Hermes Trismegistos... Perfect is what I have said of the work of the sun.' In alchemy the Unio Mystica of Sun and Moon is symbolic of the mystical union of the qualities of inner male and inner female. In Tantric thought the state of inner balance, between the energies of Sun and Moon, parallels the words of the Emerald Tablet and Jung's concept of individuation: that in the unconscious a man includes an inner female image; in a woman the image of an inner male. The union of these (conscious with unconscious) is required for psychological balance and growth, which is reflected in the geometric proportioning of the cover art itself, with the sun and moon contained within the pentagram and multiples of it (25).

It is possible that listeners sense the concept of ritual invocation unconsciously when listening to the album. In other words, power is raised by strong musical, even magical elements through the harnessing of archetypal elements. The inclusion of powerful drumming intensifies this dimension. Drums have traditionally been associated with the spiritual and magical worlds such as rites of passage, exorcisms and the invocation of spirits, and have always played a quintessential role in the music of King Crimson. Interestingly, the pentagram is itself a Golden Section form which is also included in the cover-art as multiples of five, meaning that geometric principles are active at every level of the work. The cover-art, perfectly proportioned, embodies the principle of cosmic order, reflecting the alchemical dictum, 'As above, so below'. (See Diagram 12).

Diagram 11

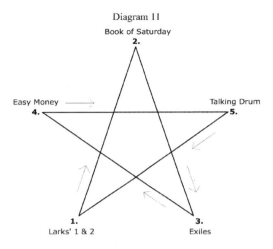

Book of Saturday
2.

Easy Money ⟶
4.

Talking Drum
5.

1.
Larks' 1 & 2

3.
Exiles

Diagram 12

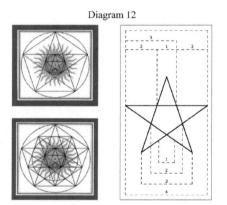

Part 2

11. Larks' Tongues In Aspic Part 1

I will concentrate on the two instrumental pieces which frame the structure and give the album its title. It was suggested by Jamie Muir who replied that the music sounded like 'Larks' tongues in Aspic' when listening to a playback of a studio instrumental take. Muir's throwaway phrase leapt out at Robert Fripp who thought it an appropriate title for the work-in-progress (26). The inner songs will be discussed mainly with reference to the two larger instrumental pieces, LTIA Parts 1 and 2.

I have already mentioned that Fripp was working with recognisably Larks' material in 1971. There is an extant 'live' recording of early versions of the material which make up the guitar solo section heard in LTIA Pt 1 - a 'performance sketch', perhaps - available as a bootleg. It is part of a piece called No. 1 Mr. Wonderful from a King Crimson Mk II concert at London's Marquee Club in 1971. This method of working with borrowed material by testing it out in different contexts has been a feature of Fripp's compositional practice. For example, North Star (found on Fripp's solo album, Exposure [1978]) later appears re-worked as Matte Kudesai on Discipline; the riff from Ooh! Mr. Fripp (from The League Of Gentlemen's Thrang Thrang Gozinbulx

[1980]) re-appears as Frame By Frame on Discipline (1981). Recent downloads of other musical material at DGM Live! have demonstrated Fripp's method of writing guitar-based material (essentially 'sonic sketches') and presenting it at rehearsals to allow participating musicians to contribute their own ideas.

LTIA Pt 1 was the first of the instrumentals to be written serving as a template, or the prima materia, for the other material heard on the album. Musical motives from it are found transformed in LTIA Pt 2, as well as being included within the song-pieces. The cyclic nature of the material seems fitting for the subject of the rite which is bound-up with the cycle of the seasons.

a) Structure, Music Types and Voice

The piece is cast in seven sections which alternates written (mostly metered) with improvised material (mostly non-metered).

1) 0:00 - Gamelan-like opening: tuned/untuned metals, improvisation, and soft, solo violin played in 'real' time.

2a) 2:54 - Anacrusis in the violin part; accumulation of the full band ensemble in metred 10/8 (5/4) (3+3+2+2 quavers); metal power-chords full band in 7/4 time; varied repeat of the same.

2b) 4:54 - Tritone-based solo guitar bridge section involving shifting metres.

3) 5:01 - Guitar, bass, drums and percussion - guitar is 'written' while the bass, drums and percussion are improvised. Metre: 11/8, then 7/8 with a metric unison section in 12/8 towards the end (5:51).

4) 6:15 - Improvised - begins on G, resolves on D.

5) 7:42 - Previous improvised section overlaps with lamenting solo violin, electric guitar (left-hand only), piano and bird-whistles; violin and zither at 9:11; rhythmic unison at 10:57 on G pentatonic (major).

6) 11:24 - Non-amplified electric guitar plus violin within accumulative texture in 10/8 (5/4) (3+3+2+2).

7) 12:27 - Climax. Point of arrival. Full band. Glockenspiels and wind chimes emerge from the full band texture at the end, crossing the sound-space, referring back to the opening.

The materials are deployed as part of a block structure where the maximum contrast is heard with acoustic instruments (metallophones/metals/zither/violin) juxtaposed with electric instruments (guitar, bass, kit drums, percussion). There is a wide dynamic range and many diverse musical materials involved in the piece including: pentatony (Section 1); metal power-chords (Section 2); fast tritone-based guitar breaks with and without the improvised anchoring material of the rhythm section; pure improvisation (Section 4); folksong-like modes with an Eastern influence (Section 5); accumulative material in the violin and the guitar parts based on octatonic scales (Sections 2 and 6); unison-like passages with false-relations (Section 7). The textural accumulations are to be heard from 2:54, 3:56 and 11:24. The violin and guitar and sometimes the percussion-based ensembles are directional bringing about dramatic climaxes reinforced by modulations. (See Diagram 13).

There is also symmetry to the structure. The tuned and untuned percussion frames the piece and the musical materials balance and elide mostly by overlapping. (See Diagram 14).

Section 1 mirrors Section 7; Section 2 mirrors Section 6; Section 3 mirrors its polar-opposite, Section 5; this leaves Section 4 as the kernel of the piece which is the explosive central improvisation. Whereas Section 1 crescendos, Section 7 diminuendos leaving the wind chimes to waft across the sound-space at the very end as a kind of after-image. The point of Golden Section is during the first half of the solo violin music on a high F natural (8:22) anticipating a silence filled-in by the sound of distant, soft rushing wind.

Diagram 13

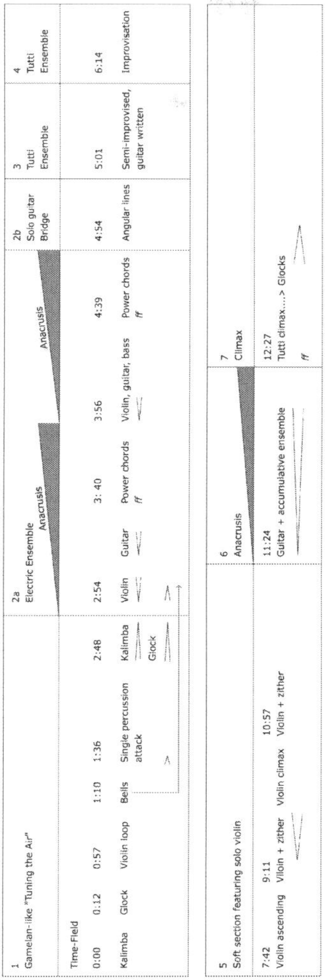
1
Gamelan-like "Tuning the Air"
Time-Field
0:00
0:12
0:57
1:10
1:36
2:48
Kalimba
Glock
Violin loop
Bells
Single percussion attack
Kalimba
Glock
2a
Electric Ensemble
Anacrusis
2:54
3:40
3:56
4:39
Violin
Guitar
Power chords
ff
Violin, guitar, bass
Anacrusis
Power chords
ff
2b
Solo guitar
Bridge
4:54
Angular lines
3
Tutti
Ensemble
5:01
Semi-improvised, guitar written
4
Tutti
Ensemble
6:14
Improvisation
5
Soft section featuring solo violin
7:42
Violin ascending
9:11
Viloin + zither
Violin climax
10:57
Violin + zither
6
Anacrusis
11:24
Guitar + accumulative ensemble
7
Climax
12:27
Tutti climax....> Glocks
ff

Diagram 14

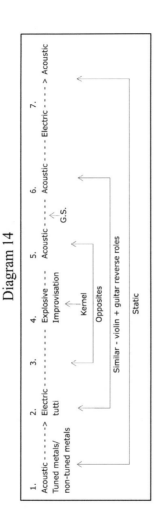

b) Pitch and Harmonic materials

LTIA Pts. 1 and 2 are based loosely around Bartók's Axis system of tonality. (See Diagram 15).

The octatonic scale used in both pieces is the Plagal version beginning on G. (See Example 4).

Pitch-classes 0, 3, 6 and 9 relate to the Tonic axis (I), while 2, 5, 8 and 11 relate to the Subdominant axis (IV). The octatonic can also be transformed to make other scales, some of which, are also utilised in the piece. (See Example 5).

This means that much of the material which make up the two extended Larks' pieces is generated from the same source. The Plagal octatonic scale is also double symmetrical, and partitioned by a tritone. (See Example 6).

I will discuss each section in some detail.

Diagram 15

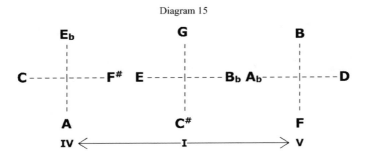

Ex 4

Ex 5

Ex 6

Section 1

This is a contrapuntal section of separate lines and events and is, in a sense, reminiscent of the beginning of The Rite Of Spring. Robert Fripp has commented: 'It might be compared to what happens in a Guitar Craft performance... "Tuning the Air"...a transition period which enables the performer and audience to sense each other, the players to re-adjust their hearing, and everyone to accommodate themselves to the moment and place. In the context of the time (1972-73), this had the effect of tweaking expectations of how a rock group might begin its evening.' (27). The listener is treated to the sounds of nature: acoustic instruments and resonance that builds leading the ear into the work. This gamelan-like 'tuning the air' involves a kalimba multi-tracked in three parts playing an A minor pentatonic collection of pitches. (See Example 7).

The glockenspiel part which then enters includes the pitches C, D, E, F and G which relate to the kalimba's A minor pentatonic material. (See Example 8).

The violin pitches are derived from the Overtone scale on G. (See Example 9).

The complete harmonic field combines pitches forming the G overtone scale, A minor Pentatonic and C major, the latter being contained within the A minor Pentatonic. (See Example 10).

Some of these pitches are duplicated and eventually give way to the upper partials of the multi-tracked bells. It is a section of pure 'nature', especially if the intervals between the pitches are seen through the prism of Fibonacci here denoted by pitch-class numbering. (See Example 11).

The kalimba also reveals a relationship with Fibonacci (Major 2nd = 2; Minor 3rd = 3; Perfect 4th = 5; Minor 6th = 8). (see Example 12).

Modal pitch-collections, based on white notes, are found in many English folksongs and serve as the basis for the closing section of the final movement of Vaughan-Williams's Pastoral Symphony where a folksong is taken into the context of an art-music work.

Ex 7

Ex 8

Ex 9

Ex 10

Ex 11

Ex 12

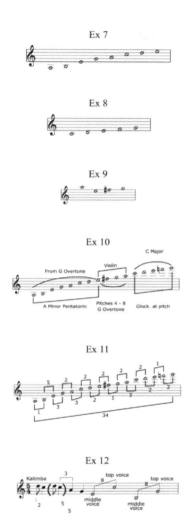

Section 2 a

The multi-tracked bells of Section 1 overlap with the violin 10/8 (5/4) at the beginning of Section 2a, which is subdivided into 3+3+2+2 quaver groupings. This section has a different kind of accumulative texture. Each instrument is introduced from the top downwards, first with solo violin at 2:54, followed by distorted electric guitar at 3:03 and, finally, percussion at 3:19 which grows in intensity reinforced by a snare drum roll at 3:34. The violin passage extends from 2:54 to 3:40 where the guitar power-chords begin. The two sections are connected by the pitches A and C natural. Section 2 is based on a Plagal octatonic scale on G. (See Example 13).

The descending guitar counterpoint, together with the accumulation of texture, creates almost unbearable tension towards the point of arrival of the power-chords at 3:40. Fripp has commented: 'This is where the powerful riff kicks-in - visually pictured as the skyscrapers of Manhattan walking sideways.' (28) The primal dawn, depicted in the opening, has given way to an aggressive urban landscape.

The metal power chords are reminiscent of those that accompany the verses during Pictures Of A City from In The Wake Of Poseidon, but here comprise shorter values ascending to Db a tritone away from G. (See Example 14).

Section 2 b

The angular solo guitar bridge section, connecting Section 2a with Section 3, is sequential and tritone-based, combining both Plagal and Authentic forms of the octatonic mode. (See Example 15).

Through the use of 0, 6, 0, 10, 4 pitch-classes Fripp is utilising the symmetrical structure of the octatonic, and with F#-C-G-C at 4:54 refers to the Plagal variety of the mode.

What does this mean for a listener? Possibly nothing at all in the abstract dimension. It does show, however, that composers often access techniques they are aware of, put them aside and then mysteriously (unconsciously) re-access them in new and inventive ways. This provides the necessary musical stimulus for the listener, moving from the abstract to the experiential mode. In the case of LTIA, this is precisely what King Crimson seem to have done, suggesting that strong archetypes are being conveyed by the musical substance.

Ex 15

Section 3

The solo guitar section provides an anacrusis into Section 3, and develops the material heard in the bridge section but this time appearing as part of an ensemble which includes bass guitar, drums and percussion. All extant recordings demonstrate that Fripp plays the same part, presumably written, while the bass and drums differ slightly each time. John Wetton has mentioned that whereas Fripp would come up with a solo guitar part the other players would then have to develop their own parts to coincide with his (29). The bass and drums of Section 3 may be considered as being 'semi-improvised' whereas Section 4 is completely improvisational, and both are centred on G. (See Example 16).

These lines are composed around position III on the bass guitar, with natural and sharpened sevenths and natural and flattened fifths: more blues-like than octatonic although blues scales can of course be derived from octatonic aggregates. The two sections stand in stark contrast to the opening modal section and the music that is yet to follow. Section 4 is loaded with brutal, primal rhythms and is a showcase for King Crimson's approach to 'live' improvisation, but here set in a studio context. The rising, tremolando chords heard in the guitar from 7:11 are octaves divided by a tritone and vertical-harmonic transpositions of the linear material found previously as part of the guitar bridge section from 4:34. There is also some similarity between Fripp's solo in section 4 and the guitar solo found in Sailor's Tale from the 1971 album, Islands.

Ex 16

Section 3: 5:00

Section 4 and Graphic Analysis

Section 4 is completely improvisational and grounded on G. Texturally, it concentrates on guitar, bass, drums and percussion serving as an anacrusis for Section 5.

Graphic analyses of middleground and background events show the directional motion of music by stripping-away surface detail. This exposes important prolongations of pitches felt to exist long after they have disappeared, yet connecting to the same pitch found at a distance in the process of the musical journey. In other words, linear unfolding is revealed at a deeper structural level in the piece by omitting diminutions, defined as localised events such as arpeggiations and passing notes heard in the foreground. In Schenkerian terms, musical material heard in the foreground often assumes less significance in the middleground and background. (For an explanation of Schenkerian musical analysis see Andrew Keeling - Musical Guide to In The Court Of The Crimson King, p. 85)

First, the middleground graph illustrates some of the main diminutions found within the fabric of LTIA Pt 1, the modal hierarchy at work in the piece, and the enduring collapse culminating in Section 7 through the 8 - 1 descent of the fundamental line. The overall line is, in essence, the descending Aeolian scale transposed to G revealed with considerable clarity in the background, yet discernible in the middleground. Secondly, it shows that Major and Minor 2nds and 3rds heard extensively in the foreground, are also present at other levels. There are two occurrences of intervallic unfoldings, through the movement of Minor 3rds in Sections 2b and 5. Thirdly, the accumulative music, heard in Section 2, is an initial ascent arriving at 8, heard as the G minor modal power chords. The initial ascent is mirrored in Section 6, although at a lower hierarchic level. Sections 5 and 6, although seemingly unconnected, serve to prolong IV (iv) C. Fourthly, falling and rising motives (i.e. A - G), heard clearly in the foreground, are represented in the harmony (ii - i; v - iv). Less prominence is given to tritones in the middleground, and these are completely absent in the background. This means that tritones, in this context, are used in a decorative manner. Fifthly, and perhaps most importantly, C is felt as a significant prolongation in the voice-leading, which is mirrored harmonically in the C major7 chord at the end of Section 3, the Plagal Cadence (IV - I [i]) at the end of Section 6, the many instances of 4th progressions found throughout the piece, and lastly, but certainly not least, in the initial ascent from C (4) to G (1) in Section 2. It is worth mentioning that chord IV is a structural ingredient within King Crimson's previous studio album, Islands (1971), and used with great effect in Formentera Lady, The Letters, Prelude: Song of the Gulls and Islands. From there, it reappears in LTIA Pt 1, Book Of Saturday and Easy Money at important structural moments. Plagal Cadences (IV - I) are found in modal contexts (due to the absence of the strong leading-note in chord V) such as Anglican and French choral music.

I suggest that 4 and IV, 1-4/4-1 progressions and cadences connected with it (Plagal) represent the feminine aspect of the work contained by and, paradoxically, containing the main masculine structural pillars of G modal minor. There are parallels here with the underlying cosmological signifiers found at the root of the work. Finally, the background graph demonstrates that LTIA Pt 1 is, indeed, a large-scale embellishment of an underlying harmonic progression (i - v - IV - iv - i - I), and a hugely expanded cadence allowing us a glimpse into the organic properties of the piece. (See Examples 17 and 18).

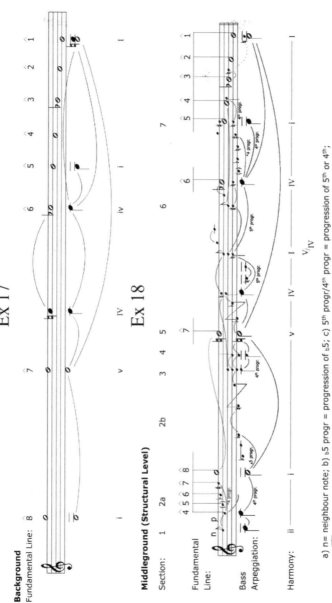

Ex 17

Background

Fundamental Line: 8̂ 7̂ 6̂ 5̂ 4̂ 3̂ 2̂ 1̂

i v IV iv i I

Ex 18

Middleground (Structural Level)

Section:	1	2a	2b	3	4	5	6	7

Fundamental
Line: 4̂ 5 6 7 8̂   7̂   6̂   5̂ 4̂ 3̂ 2̂ 1̂

Bass
Arpeggiation: n p   4th progr.   ♭5 progr.   4th progr.   9th progr.   5th progr.   ♭5 progr.   4th progr.

Harmony: ii — i — v — IV — i — I — IV — i
                                        V_IV

a) n= neighbour note; b) ♭5 progr = progression of ♭5; c) 5th progr/4th progr = progression of 5th or 4th;
d) 𝅗𝅥 = connections between fundamental line; e) ⌣ = prolongational units, connecting pitches on a large scale
f) = registral transfer

Section 5

Suddenly light emerges from the tension of Section 4 with the resolution of Section 5. It is a moment which conveys emerging 'spirit' as though escaping from (urban) matter, and important in the context of the piece where the natural voice of musical folk tradition is heard. There is great aural clarity in this much reduced, rather static section comprising violin, soft electric guitar (left-hand only on the fretboard) accompanied by zither and bird-calls. From 7:45 to 8:22 there is a rising line in the violin taking the range from A (a Major 6th above middle C) to F natural, a Minor 13th higher.

The guitar part, reinforced by rapid piano arpeggiations, plays Major 7th chords divided by a tritone which refers back to the arpeggio found at 6:09. (See Example 19).

The chords ascend from 7:42 to one a Minor 3rd higher at 8:12. (See Example 20).

The chords at 7:42 in part, are picked-up from the C major7th chord found at 6:11 which creates a link with the IV axis and the pitches drawn from the G octatonic scale. An ascending Minor

3rd is also found derived from the guitar bridge passage in Section 2a. (See Example 21).

The subsequent subsection from 8:35 is cadenza-like picking-up the Ab in the violin line from 7:50. The Ab's of this section are more pronounced and probably drawn from a combination of the Plagal and Authentic forms of the octatonic, although it is possible that the Japanese 'soft scale' is being referenced. (see Example 22).

These lines extend upwards to the high E natural at 8:58, and the music becomes centred on C mixolydian. (See Example 23)

At 9:11 the zither plays tremolando B, A and G natural outlining a G major collection which underpins a folksong-like dance in the violin part at 9:20. This seems to be a reference to Vaughan Williams's The Lark Ascending (1914) for solo violin and orchestra. The reference is heightened by the bird-whistles (larks?) which hover in the background of the first part of the section, and the arching shape of the line. From letter E in The Lark Ascending there is a lilting dance rhythm which seems to be the main point of reference for the violin line in LTIA Pt 1 from 9:20 onwards. There is also a section of Perfect 4ths and Perfect 5ths at letter S (compare to LTIA Pt 1 - 10:11) combined with Minor 3rds found as part of the linearity. Both pieces include violin tremolando. However, there are no direct quotations of The Lark Ascending to be found in LTIA Pt 1, but the reference remains in terms of the open rhapsodic form. The many Major 2nds, 3rds, Perfect 4ths and 5ths are also Fibonacci-based (2, 3, 5, 8). As a comparison, the intervals found in the opening Cadenza of the Vaughan Williams piece can be seen in Example 24. The zither section, from 10:57, also points to the possible influence of Eastern musics with its shifting metres of 6, 4 and 3 crotchets. David Cross has recently said although he can't remember consciously listening to the Vaughan Williams piece, he must have come across it somewhere.

Section 6

This section is a recapitulation of the accumulative character of Section 2 although, here, the role of the violin and the guitar is reversed. It is constructed around the IV axis, introduced on an unamplified electric guitar which overlaps with the acoustic quality of Section 5, and creates a pivot into Section 7 which is a combination of electric and acoustic instruments. (See Diagram 16).

It is also a musical backdrop for the spoken-voice: a recording of the BBC radio play, Gallowglass by John and Willy Maley. This deals with the passing of a death sentence, an apt choice of material for LTIA considering the sacrificial victim of ancient Spring rites whose spilled blood both appeases the deities and ensures a successful harvest. The IV axis is operative throughout this section and related to an octatonic scale based on C. From 11: 24 - 11:41 pitch-classes 11, 2, 3, 6 and 8 are referenced. (See Diagram 17).

Whereas from 11:44 to 12:19 the following pitch-classes are utilised. (See Example 25).

The shift of pitch and register takes into account the increasing tension reinforced by the accumulation of the voices from 12:07.

Diagram 16

Section 5	Section 6					Section 7
	11:24	11:36	11:41	11:45	12:07	12:21	12:27

Section 5 | Section 6
Violin [
Zither]

11:24 — Unamplified electric guitar - - - - - >
11:36
11:41 — Violin - - - - - >
11:45 — Bass guitar - - - - >
12:07
12:21 — Violin A - Bb / Snare drum / more voices..........
12:27 — Full Ensemble

Female spoken voice.......... voices gain in intensity.............. male spoken voice + 173

bar: 143 152 154 165

ppp —————————

To be hung by the neck.....DEAD
ff

Diagram 17

11 - 24 ff.

Guitar

Ex 25

Section 7

The texture builds into Section 7 (12:27 and following) and introduces the open texture of rhythm guitar crosspicking a chord of G minus the third (eventually adding Bb), contrary-motion violin against de-tuned lead guitar and bass guitar, with glockenspiels at the rear of the mix. The point of arrival is affirmed by the word 'dead!' spoken exactly on the downbeat at 12:27. The music is in a dark G minor mode based on two combined forms of the octatonic scale, and planted firmly on the I axis. It is the Nigredo stage of the piece where the full impact of the death sentence is felt, accompanied by the mourning and rapidly praying voices heard as part of the texture. The three muttering voices are Jamie Muir's, David Cross' and Bill Bruford's reading any literature to hand in the studio at the time. Out of this musical darkness emerges the light of the glockenspiels based on Minor 3rds (B and D; D and F) but transformed into the major mode by the Tonic G in the guitar part. The glockenspiels extend the range of the guitar upwards.

d) Motives as 'Scintillae' and their distribution

The essential musical motives, which can be read as scintillae (sparks), or seeds using an alchemical metaphor, are widely distributed around the fabric of LTIA. By taking the Alchemical Opus as a metaphor, transformation of materials is the central feature in LTIA. In other words, it is as though the 'base metal' of LTIA Pt 1 is transformed into the 'gold' of LTIA Pt 2.

1) Riffs: the material in Section 3 of LTIA Pt 1 at 5:50 is taken into the fabric of LTIA Pt 2 at 0:08 but are rhythmically transformed. (See Example 26).

2) Both versions are also transformed by transposition and by sequential means. It is as though the germ which appeared as a passing idea in LTIA Pt 1 is used at a higher structural level within the fabric of Pt 2. Here it is presented whole, fully-grown and capable of further development, in an episodic and linear form connecting one section of chords with another, as well as forcing modulation. The pitch material is derived from the Authentic form of the octatonic scale, but includes a C natural and an F# from the Plagal version. (See Example 27).

Ex 26

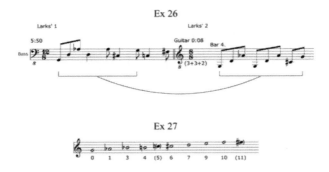

Ex 27

e) Rising Lines During Accumulative Passages

LTIA Pt 1 includes passages of ascending material found in the violin and guitar parts of the accumulative music that usually leads to an enormous climax. These are heard during Section 2 at 2:54 and in Section 6 at 11:27. The material is octatonically derived. (See Example 28).

This material is transformed into the sustained, lyrical material of LTIA Pt 2 at 0:46, 2:31 and 4:46 which is extended on each occurrence. In both pieces the material triggers a climax. It can be seen from both a) and b) that two interlocking tritones are present, which gradually takes the music upwards: in a) the tritones are C - Gb and Eb - A, and in b) A - D# and C - F#.

Ex 28

f) Octatonic and Pentatonic

The distribution of pitch materials within the fabric of LTIA is based on three clearly differentiated types: a) octatonic; b) minor pentatonic; c) major pentatonic.

a) Octatonic: these areas are often, although not exclusively, reserved for the rising accumulative sections as well as for some of the riffs. Interlocking tritones are also included in these collections, which I have previously discussed. (See Example 29).

The main heartbeat bass riff in The Talking Drum is also tritone-based. (See Example 30).

Many tritones are found within the fabric of LTIA Pt 1, especially in the earlier guitar solo in the bridge section from 4:54.

b) Minor Pentatonic: there are many examples of modal material found throughout the work. Rock music, in general, is saturated with 0, 2, 3, 5 collections and, in the case of LTIA, examples of 0, 3, 5 and 0, 3, 5, 6 are also to be found. I am not stating a case for modal pitch collections of this type being exclusive to the work under consideration, but as they are included it is interesting to see how an initial seed is distributed. For example, the opening of LTIA Pt 1 includes the following. (See Example 31). Moonchild, from In The Court of the Crimson King, also utilises a minor pentatonic pitch collection on A.

Similar collections are also to be found in the metal chords of Pt 1, the vocal parts of Book Of Saturday and Exiles and the guitar part of The Talking Drum. They are also Fibonacci-based in terms of intervals. (See Example 32).

c) Major Pentatonic: as compared to earlier King Crimson albums sections of major pentatony are found less in LTIA. It is a feature of In The Wake Of Poseidon being used to begin, partition and close the work. In the case of LTIA a major pentatonic collection is used to generate the material of Exiles. (See Examples 33 and 34).

The vocal part of Exiles is a re-ordering of pitches from the opening mellotron material which is a re-working of Mantra, an earlier King Crimson piece found on the 'live' Epitaph collection (DGM 9607, 1997). Violinist David Cross wrote the song's main melody which follows the introduction. (See Example 35). The melody of the verses is also fashioned from the violin material.

It is possible to include a distibutional diagram of some of the important melodic motives demonstrating how they are taken into the vocal parts of each song. It is as though Section 1 of LTIA Pt 1 provides a 'motive-pool' of sorts to generate material for vocal and instrumental ideas found throughout the work. In this way it is as though the scintillae evolve from their origins as seeds in the context of Section 1, into fully-grown melodic phrases elsewhere. (See Example 36).

Ex 29

Ex 30

Ex 31

Ex 32

Ex 33

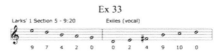

Ex 34

Ex 35

12. Larks' Tongues In Aspic Part 2

LTIA Pt 2 is an exciting and vigorous round-dance. Balancing with LTIA Pt 1, it can be heard as the moment of rebirth rising from the death at the end of the first piece.

LTIA Pt 2 is the only piece on the album credited to Robert Fripp as sole composer. Rhythmically speaking it is influenced by The Rite Of Spring through the prism of Bartók (Bulgarian Dance No. 153) and Jimi Hendrix (Foxy Lady and Purple Haze). It also represents the direction in which Fripp's musical direction was subsequently to take. There is a direct connection with Fracture (1973), Red (1974), Breathless (1977), Vroom (1994) and the Larks' Tongues in Aspic pieces, No. 3 (1984) and No. 4 (2000) in terms of the compositional and instrumental techniques found in all of them. FraKctured and EleKctric (from The ConstruKction of Light and The Power to Believe respectively) might also be considered in the same context. (See Appendix for an analysis of Red).

a) Structure

The piece is 186 bars long if the D major coda is taken into the reckoning, or 163 bars without it. It is difficult to say, without having access to Fripp's original score (assuming it exists), if the coda is an improvised unmetred section, but I suspect it arouse mainly through improvisation and by manipulating the final sustained chord through studio techniques. Whichever is the case means there are implications for the positioning of events by use of Golden Section. The piece is in five sections.

> 1) 0:00 - 1:48 (bars 1-43)
> 2) 1:50 - 3:40 (bars 44-88)
> 3) 3:41 - 4:44 (bars 89-132)
> 4) 4:45 - 5:55 (bars 133-163)
> 5) 5:57 - 7:03 (bars 163-186)

The first half of the piece (0:00 - 3:40 [bars 1-88]) is made from three types of material, which are all connected by the 10/8 (5/4) rhythm. Each type of material is different: i) metal chords; ii) angular riff; iii) sustained, lyrical and accumulative. (See Example 37).

The angular riff (ii) and the sustained lyrical material (iii) are the scintillae (seeds/sparks) picked-up from LTIA Pt 1 and, in this context are presented as whole creating unity in the work. The three kinds of material may be represented graphically. (See Diagram 18).

The linear riff (ii) connects the strident metal chords. It also effects modulation connecting to the sustained lyrical material (iii) which features the violin. The latter takes the music upwards, via Minor thirds, picked up from LTIA Pt 1, and is transformed by expansion. It is also derived from octatonic sources. (See Example 38).

Each sustained lyrical passage leads to an event that is felt as a sub-climax: either as a D7 chord or as often-repeated and hammered open fifths on D. The following graphic representation shows a gradual dynamic and textural accumulation increased by the orgasmic utterances, produced by the manipulation of air-filled balloons, within the texture just before 2:42 (bar 64) to 3:41 (bar 88). (See Diagram 19).

The central section of LTIA Pt2 (3:41 [bar 89] to 4:44 [bar 132]) introduces metal parallel fourth power-chords in the guitar, underpinned by bass guitar, recalling the power-chords found in LTIA Pt 1. The wild violin solo from 3:59 (bar 100) to 4:44 (bar 132) is placed at the point of Golden Section (Fibonacci 8:13), and because of this is clearly felt to be the focal point (point of G.S. - 163 x 8 -:- 13 = 100). At 4:24 (bar 118) the electric guitar plays a rhythm in 10/8 (5/4) which is set against the rhythm in the bass and drums to create a polyrhythm. This triggers the sustained lyrical music at 4:45 (bar 133) where the two strands of the polyrhythm coincide. David Cross' violin solo is highly significant. First, because of its mainly tremolando gestures and short manic bursts of activity it picks up from the previous section's percussion part which utilises air-filled balloons. Secondly, it prepares the section of the guitar and bass polyrhythm which extends to the complex interplay between the kit-drums and the percussion where Jamie Muir is heard playing kit for the first time in the piece.

LTIA Pt 2 is sectionalised into short tableaux-like blocks and can be regarded as a network of braids which overlap and interact with one another. The music theorist Edward T. Cone (30) has called this process 'stratification'. (See Diagram 20).

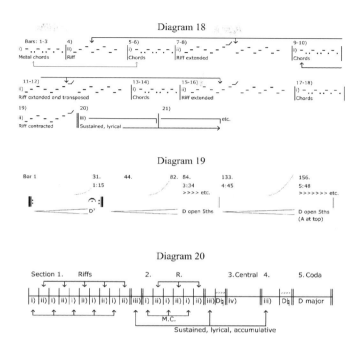

Diagram 18

Bars: 1-3	4)	5-6)	7-8)	9-10)
i)	ii)	i)	ii)	i)
Metal chords	Riff	Chords	Riff extended	Chords

11-12)	13-14)	15-16)	17-18)
ii)	i)	ii)	i)
Riff extended and transposed	Chords	Riff extended	Chords

19)
ii) Riff contracted

20)
iii) Sustained, lyrical

21)
etc.

Diagram 19

Bar 1

31.   44.   82. 84.   133.   156.
         1:15   3:34   4:45   5:48
                          >>>> etc.   >>>>>>> etc.

D⁷   D open 5ths   D open 5ths
(A at top)

Diagram 20

Section 1.   Riffs   2.   R.   3. Central 4.   5. Coda

i) ii) i) ii) i) ii) i) ii) i) ii) iii) i) ii) i) ii) i) ii) iii) D♮ iv) | iii) | D♮ | D major

M.C.

Sustained, lyrical, accumulative

i)= metal chords   ii)= riffs   iii)= sustained, lyrical, accumulative   iv) central power chords

b) Harmony

Harmony plays both a colouristic but mainly functional role in the music of King Crimson. It is used structurally to generate tension in the background over long spans. LTIA Pt 2 demonstrates the way in which Dominant (V) harmony is used as a structural goal and undergoes prolongation at the point of its arrival. Of course, points of arrival on the Dominant are nothing new. In many classical sonata structures recapitulation sections are usually preceded by lengthy stretches of Dominant harmony, and in twelve-bar blues structures V is felt to be significant. There is enormous tension generated both by anticipation of the dominant and its prolongation in LTIA Pt 2. The final D major chord of the coda is felt to be the resolution of the piece and a kind of 'farewell' signal. It is also the final long-term resolution to the A minor mode found at the beginning of LTIA Pt 1. (See Example 39).

The D major chord is reminiscent of the second inversion found in the guitar part at the end of Sailor's Tale from Islands (1971). The resonance from the chord which fades-out during bar 176 (6: 32), fades back in from bar 179 (6:40) and gradually decays to the end, owing something to the piano chord heard in the coda of A

Day In The Life on The Beatles' Sgt Pepper's Lonely Hearts Club Band (1967).

i) Metal Chords: these are added-note in type - two modal, two sevenths with flattened-fifths. (See Example 40). To reinforce the brutality a C is added to create piled-up fourths (G, C, F, Bb).

These chords, generated partly by guitar fingering, trigger the linear unison riffs which, in turn, connect to the subsequent chords.

ii) Riffs: these are picked-up from LTIA Pt 1 and, in the context of Pt 2, are presented in a transformed version. They are guitar-generated and narrow across adjacent frets. (See Example 41).

As with other material the riffs are derived from octatonic sources. Robert Fripp has written: 'The octatonic (double symmetrical) scale seemed to me, as a rock guitarist, very obvious: the scale was both major and minor, or straight and "blue". To include both forms of the third as equally legitimate in a scale of eight notes wasn't a very great conceptual leap' (31). The riffs appear during the first half of the piece and disappear at 2:29 (bar 59). It is as though their purpose has been exhausted, particularly after the power chords of the central section at 3:42 (bar 89). The riffs cover the twelve pitches of a chromatic scale, and serve as an example of a fairly free adaptation of a Serial note-row.

The following example shows that pitch-classes 7, 3 and 11 create an augmented triad. (See Example 42).

In turn these pitches are also included in the combined Plagal and Authentic octatonic scales. (See Example 43).

The riffs are also transformed from 0:15 - 0:17 (bars 7 - 8) and subsequently through additive and subtractive rhythmic cells. I will discuss this during the section on rhythm.

Modulation such as this is often found in jazz, as well as in the music of Mussorgsky and Scriabin, especially as the pivot pitch (C natural) is common to the chords, and the Gb (of the Ab7) is re-spelt as F# in the D major chord. The music seems to be a more intuitive reworking of the pure octatony found in LTIA Pt 1 from

2:54 to 3:39. (See Example 44)

The C natural, which is an inside pedal-pitch, provides the music with fluid tertian chordal transitions.

iii) Sustained Lyrical Accumulative Music: added alongside the modal and Dominant-type chords are new chords in the softer sustained violin-dominated passages of lyrical music. This music has a tendency to resolve the tension of the metal chords and the riffs and is the first time the violin plays expressively in the piece. The accompanying chords can be described as follows:

> 0:46 (bar 20) - G11 (minus B natural)
> 0:57 (bar 24) - Bb11 (minus D natural)
> 1:02 (bar 26) - Bb13 (minus D natural)
> 1:07 (bar 28) - Ab major
> 1:13 (bar 30) - Ab7
> 1:15 (bar 31) - D

(See Example 45).

The Ab chord becomes Ab7 at 1:13 (bar 30) before moving to D at 1:15 (bar 31). (See Example 46). Fripp was to explore this kind of chording on his album Exposure (1979).

The music of this section is characterised by falling Major 3rds and rising Major 2nds and although, in some ways, it resolves the brutality of the metal chords and the angularity of the riffs, the gradual effect is one of mounting intensity increased by the irregular phrase lengths. This is demonstrated from bar 60 (2:31) to 88 (3:40)

> 4 bars - bar 60 (2:31) to 63 (2:39)
> 2 bars - bar 64 (2:42) to 65 (2:44)
> 4 bars - bar 66 (2:47) to 65 (2:55)
> 2 bars - bar 70 (2:57) to 65 (3:00)
> 2 bars - bar 72 (3:03) to 65 (3:05)
> 2 bars - bar 74 (3:08) to 65 (3:11)
> 3 bars - bar 76 (3:13) to 65 (3:21)
> 3 bars - bar 79 (3:21) to 65 (3:26)
> 2 bars - bar 82 (3:29) to 65 (3:32)

The section culminates in five bars of hammered open-fifth

chording from 84 (3:35) to bar 88 (3:40) felt as a point of arrival.

I will discuss the music of the central section iv) in the following section on rhythm.

Ex 39

Ex 40

Ex 41

Ex 42

Ex 43

Ex 44

Ex 45

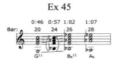

Ex 46

c) Rhythm

The rhythm of LTIA Pt 2 is based on complex and, often, shifting metres, which are sometimes additive and sometimes subtractive. The 10/8 (5/4) metre that begins the piece bears some similarity to Auguries of Spring from The Rite Of Spring and Bartok's Bulgarian Dance No. 153 from Mikrokosmos VI and, even, the rhythmic underlay of the theme music for the TV series 'Mission Impossible'. The bars are subdivided into rhythmic cells of quavers with 10/8 (5/4) as the governing metre: 3 + 3 + 2 + 2. The following example shows how the metres are associated with the metal power-chords and riffs. The metres reinforce the pitch and harmonic materials in the process of stratification. (See Example 47).

The chords largely appear in complex metres (10/8 [5/4] - 3 + 3 + 2 + 2) whereas the riffs are set within more regular metres (8/8 [4/4] - 3 + 3 + 2). The sustained lyrical music beginning at 0:46 (bar 20) is in 11/8 (3 + 3 + 3 + 2) although the 5/4 metre is re-established in the following bar. Listeners become aware of the main pulse of the metal power-chords (dotted crotchet, dotted crotchet, crotchet, crotchet) as a kind of lurching dance rhythm. The rhythm of the brutal central section (3:42 and following ([bar

89 - 132) is slightly different. From 3:41 (bar 89) there is an example of the re-distribution of accents which trip-up listener expectations. (See Example 48).

It can also be heard as: (See Example 49). Or: (See Example 50). It is later transformed from bar 94 to 96: (See Example 51). On 'The Night Watch' (King Crimson 'live' at the Amsterdam Concertgebouw November 23rd 1973 - DGM CD 97072) it is possible to hear the section from bar 97 (3:55ff.) in the following way: (See Example 52).

These chords prepare the manic violin solo at 5:59 (bar 100 and following) which is positioned at the place of Golden Section, with a polymetre occurring from bar 118 (4:24). While the bass continues the previous rhythm (6/8 + 6/8 + 4/8), the guitar plays a transposition of its 10/8 material heard in the section of sustained, lyrical, accumulative music. It is an event where all the textural elements seem to be in conflict. (See Example 53).

The purpose of the polyrhythm is to trigger the recapitulation of the 10/8 (5/4) sustained lyrical music heard at 4:45 (bar 133), and the ascending violin glissando. Polymetres are often found in the music of Stravinsky (Three Pieces for String Quartet - I), Bartók (String Quartet No. 3 - Seconda Parte) and Britten (Festival Te Deum). In the case of Bartók's Third String Quartet it is used to trigger important motivic material, and in the Stravinsky to set a mechanical texture in motion. LTIA PT 2 includes a similar rhythm to that found found in Bartók's Bulgarian Dance No. 6 (Mikrokosmos VI - No. 153): (See Example 54)

The first bar of LTIA Pt 2 may also be regarded as an extension of the 3 + 3 + 2 rhythm of the Bartók to 3 + 3 + 2 + 2. In terms of its rhythmic vitality LTIA Pt 2 is also close to Stravinsky's The Augurs of Spring - Dances of the Young Girls from The Rite Of Spring. The chugging string rhythms, here, are set in 2/4 but utilise irrational accenting to heighten the sexual energy of the dance. (See Example 55).

Fripp's harmonic language, in LTIA Pt 2, is close to the Stravinsky. The chord in The Augurs of Spring is spelt as Eb7/Fb and tritonically connected through the Fb and Bb. Stravinsky's chording also owes something to two connected octatonic collections. (See Example 56).

Bartók was interested in odd and even metres, often writing movements in three times three eighths or two times two eighths (Sonata for Two Pianos and Percussion). This dimension of rhythmic structuring is used in LTIA Pt 2 as we have seen. Even rhythms are also distributed in the work, initially derived from the odd rhythms of the first section of LTIA Pt 1. As I have previously suggested, this serves as a kind of 'pool' or container - a primal swamp, even - from which the work's materials are built. (See Example 57).

The precedents for the odd/even metres of LTIA Pt. 2 may be found in the 42nd At Treadmill section during Pictures Of A City (In The Wake Of Poseidon) with its 3+3+2+2 (+2+2+2) (4:49), and The Battle Of Glass Tears (Lizard), 3+3+3+3+2+2 (14:20). Odd and even metres are also found during the metal-inspired The Great Deceiver (Starless And Bible Black) 3+3+3+3+2+2 (0: 17) and Frame By Frame (Discipline) 2+2+3 (1:08) with its, essentially, Minimalist concerns. Primal rhythm is at the basis of King Crimson, whether jazz - which King Crimson Mk I certainly is - or Indian raga put through the prism of Steve Reich and rock as the Mk IV version of the band demonstrates to great effect. However, it seems to me that fragments of the early jazz rhythms found in some of the music of the Mk I version remains, but is foregrounded in LTIA Pts 1 and 2, and combined with the Bartók and Stravinsky influences, rather than appearing just as rhythmic foundation. It is interesting to note that Fripp's penchant for jazz is found on Travis and Fripp's Thread (Panegyric, 2008) and Cross' classical leanings are heard on Cross and Keeling's English Sun (Noisy Records, 2009). John Wetton's direct approach to song-writing, along with his guitaristic bass technique, was well placed in the context of Asia and Bill Bruford's jazz feel and meticulous rhythmic precision is heard to full effect on such albums as Gradually Going Tornado and the extensive output of Earthworks.

A precedent for the odd and even meters, as well as shifting-metres, found in LTIA are also present in The Beatles' Good Day Sunshine from Revolver (1966), where two 3+3+2 quavers underpin the two-bar phrasing in the chorus. The final chorus alternates 3+3+2 with 3+3+1 (7/8) leading to the final imitative playout. Robert Fripp has expressed his enthusiasm for the music of The Beatles on many occasions.

Ex 55

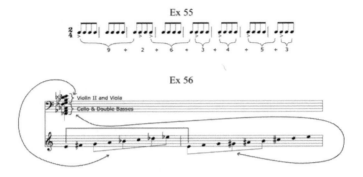

Ex 56

Ex 57

d) Rhythm Continued

i) Percussion

Bill Bruford's kit-drum and Jamie Muir's percussion playing are also highly inventive. A case-in-point is the closed to open hi-hat triplets, heard in the kit part, as part of the lyrical sustained music. The triplets progressively increase from the end towards the beginning of the bars from 21 onwards. In bar 21 the triplet unit falls on beat nine; in bar 22 it falls on beat eight; by bar 23 it falls on beat six. In the subsequent section of sustained, lyrical music the hi-hat rhythm has moved up further to the beginning of the bar. (See Example 58). This kind of rhythmic displacement is deployed by Fripp in the guitar part of God's Monkey on the Sylvian and Fripp album The First Day (1993).

Initially Jamie Muir's percussion playing is reserved to reinforce the downbeats of the sections of metal power-chords. This involves the use of metals, both indefinite-pitch and near-tuned. The riffs tend to be taken by the kit drums allowing the force of the percussion to re-emerge for the power-chords. However, during LTIA Pt 2 Muir's percussion undergoes a transformative journey beginning with: metals (bar 2 0:02), temple blocks (bar 12 [0:27]) and hi-hat (bar 16 [0:36] 'air': games-whistle (bar 40 [1:40]), balloons (bar 63 [2:39] to bar 88 [3:40]; kit (bar 97 [3:

55] to the end).

Ex 58

ii) Rhythmic 'Five-ness'

The most basic form of five-ness - the occult signifier which is encoded into the work at a background level - is expressed rhythmically in the many examples of 10/8 (5/4) metres and 3+2 (=5) quaver groupings. As I have discussed previously, five is associated with such phenomena as the Fibonacci sequence of numbers and the pentagram.

Five semi-quaver groups are hammered home with great force in bar 46 creating an intense polyrhythmic texture of guitar, on the one hand, and the bass and drums on the other. The Db is sounded in the bass five times. (See Example 59).

A more localised form of dual metre is apparant in the kit-drums from bar 40 - 42 (1:40 - 1:42) where 2's (in the ride cymbal) are layered over 3's in the bass drum and snare.

Again, the five-ness, here 2 against 3 (=5) is heightened by rhythmic means, but also combines the 3 + 2 quaver groupings in one part. (See Example 60).

The ultimate example of even (2) against odd (3) is heard in the polyrhythm from bar 138 (4:58) to 140 (5:03), where the kit-drums play in 2/4 against the 10/8 metre in the other instruments. (See Example 61).

It also marks a transition where the texture is more legato, providing a moment of calm between the chaos of the previous section and the gradually building tension towards the end.

Five-ness is also involved in the hammered rhythmic-unison of open-fifths heard from bar 84 (3:34) - 88 (3:40), where there are five bars each including five even quavers. (See Example 62).

Further examples of this occult signifier are heard during the polyrhythm of the middle section where the 10/8 (5/4) of the guitar part, is combined with five complete 6/8 + 6/8 + 4/8 phrases heard in bass part (see Score, bar 118 (4:24) - 132 (4:44).

Ex. 59

Ex 60

Ex 61

Ex 62

The Score of Larks' Tongues in Aspic Part 2 (1973)

(transcribed by Andrew Keeling)

Davis Cross, Violin - played acoustically, close-miked.

Robert Fripp, Guitar - Gibson Les Paul 'overdriven' through Hi-Watt 100 watt amplifier, and one 4x12 cabinet.

John Wetton, Bass - Fender Precision through Fuzz-Wah Pedal and Hi-Watt 100 watt amplifier and two 4x12 cabinets.

Bill Bruford, Kit-Drums - Ludwig/Hayman drums, Paiste cymbals.

Jamie Muir, Percussion - Premier/Ajax drums. Many and varied woods, metals and effects.

(The main metre has largely been written in 10/8 but may be thought of as 5/4 divided into 3+3+2+2 quavers).

Larks' Tongues In Aspic - Part Two

Robert FRIPP

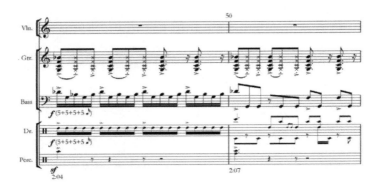

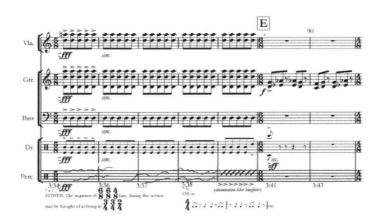

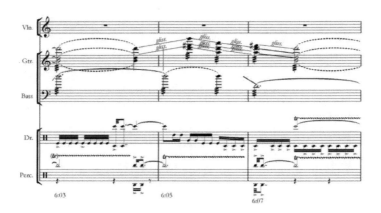

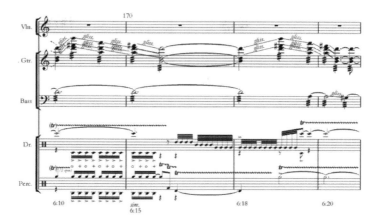

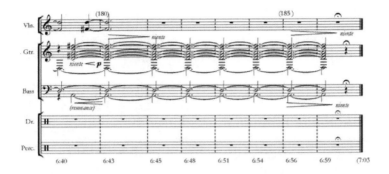

12. Conclusion

On the surface LTIA offers little in the way of verbal cues to a specific frame of reference. Without the information that David Cross and Robert Fripp have recently divulged it is possible that many different interpretations could be applied to the work. However, it is interesting that cosmological signifiers are encoded into it as hidden elements. In other words, the rite - sexual, Tantric and other magical levels - are symbolised in the work's architecture both aurally (in the music) and visually (in the cover art).

LTIA epitomises the shift away from the polystylism of previous classical progressive rock into a more unified, less heterogeneous approach. This is also associated with the decline of countercultural statements as a dominant force in the music of the late 1960's and early '70's along with the anticipation of styles of the late 1970's. The concept of LTIA (and I am slightly reticent in using this term) is a very different one from, say, the concept albums of Emerson, Lake and Palmer and Yes. Although it seems that on the surface King Crimson Mk III dispense with jazz elements, almost tentatively, I suspect this remains in the substructures of some of the pieces submerged in both harder-edged rock and classical influences. Any influence from the art-music tradition is used for the purpose of its compositional techniques rather than as pure quotation. It is as though King Crimson Mk III challenge the very foundations of the generation of the so-called 'Progressive' bands, in particular the references to traditional high-art at the core of the genre. Even though the album includes two large unified multi-sectional pieces, King Crimson steer a world away from such archetypal progressive acts like ELP, Yes, Genesis or Gentle Giant. In some ways this version of King Crimson define the post-progressive proto-punk unit that eventually spawned the 1974 album, Red, influencing bands such as Rush, and recently referenced by Radiohead (Just Found [The Bends, 1995]), cited as a favourite of Nirvana's Kurt Cobain, and the angular riff-generated bands such as Don Caballero. In 2009 progressive metal band, Dream Theatre, included a version of Larks' Tongues in Aspic Part 2 on their most successful album to date, Black Clouds and Silver Linings.

Robert Fripp has said: 'Progressive as a term confines King Crimson to an unpleasant prison and generates unfortunate expectations in the audience/public domain. Progressive, as a term, had a relevance at the beginning only: in my view King Crimson defined the genre, but when the term became a label it moved on to become a straightjacket, and then a form of insult.' (32) He has, however, recently revised his view. (DGM Playback, Air Studios, London, Oct. 2009) However, the King Crimson of LTIA retain some stylistic elements common to the original 1969 line-up, but challenge the precedent set by that group in terms of timbre (substituting violin for saxes), composition (the music of LTIA became even more angular), lyrics (the denuding of countercultural references) and improvisation. For a start, there is the inclusion of Jamie Muir's extrovert percussion style and, secondly, the harder-edged approach of Robert Fripp's playing on this album as compared to previous King Crimson albums. John Wetton's virtuoso bass guitar style owes something to Chris Squire's role in Yes, and Fripp has referred to Wetton as 'a guitar player, rather than purely a bass player' (33). David Cross contributes expressivity and originality, while Bill Bruford's virtuosity distinguishes the band from its close contemporaries. After Muir's departure, King Crimson became less dependent on theatrical exploration. Of course, it could be claimed that that there had been a successive stripping-back of extramusical thinking in the band since Peter Sinfield's departure in 1971, a tendency which is observed fully on Red (1974) and Discipline (1980-81), and leading ultimately to The ConstruKction Of Light (2000). Also, in terms of instrumentation, this King Crimson continued to use two onstage mellotrons. The keyboard (tape) instrument normally associated with Progressive rock, is used sparingly on LTIA and it must be said that King Crimson never exploited it other than where song structures (or improvisations) demanded its presence.

Robert Fripp has the ability to gather together the right players at the right time allowing the 'voice' of King Crimson to work on and through them. This otherness utters-forth as a powerful presence in Larks' Tongues In Aspic, working through the combination of the players and of opposites - musico-cosmological - which lie at the centre of this timeless work.

Fripp has commented: 'Nor can I accept that this benevolent power (the "good fairy") suddenly came to an end in December 1969. Although the sufficient conditions for the Crimson creative process to fully come to life had difficulty in getting re-established.... LTIA Pt 2 suggests to me that it did' (34).

Finally, David Cross has said: 'There was a real mix of improvising, arranging and composition going on. The most important aspect was saying "yes" to each other and not blocking ideas that might be out of our personal comfort zones. I remember putting pencil to paper for the LTIA Pt. 1 cadenza and creating a melodic realization of Robert's opening chord sequence for its reprise, but most of my contributions arose from improvisations free and otherwise (35)." This approach to the spontaneous lies at the root of LTIA, as a manifestation of universal energies found in nature.

Appendix - An Analysis Of Red

Red is an instrumental piece scored for electric guitar (multi-tracked X3), bass guitar, cello and drums and included on King Crimson's seventh studio album, Red. The musicians concerned are Robert Fripp (guitar), John Wetton (bass), Bill Bruford (drums) and a session cellist. It is one of Fripp's more muscular pieces, in particular the deployment of open strings and heavily attacked and syncopated bass and drums underlines this aspect. It also illustrates the composer's interest in musical techniques which are not necessarily found in the field of rock music.

The piece is cast in five main sections:

1.   Introduction - a series of ascending Octatonic scales played in octaves by two guitars, and supported by large open chords in guitar 3, with the bass and drums;
2.   a 'refrain' section 'on' E;
3.   middle section of repeated dyads in the electric guitar with syncopated octaves in the cello and bass;
4.   recapitulation of section 2 ('refrain-like material');
5.   recapitulation of section 1 (the ascending Octatonic scales).

The piece may be thought of as a series of relationships closely connected with the opening/ascending scales. These are Octatonic type 'a' scales, which alternate tones with semitones:

D#-E#-F#-G#-A-B-C-D (bars 1-2);
B-C#-D-E-F-G-Ab-Bb (bars 5-6);

Included within this above collection of pitches is a series of tritone intervals, D# (Eb)-A in particular, which is taken into the large-scale harmonic framework of Red. For example, the D#(Eb)-A motive is included within the second 7/8 sub-section when the bass guitar alternates A natural (over two bars) with its tritonic opposite D#/Eb. The rising Minor 3rd chords, heard in the first section, are also found in the first Octatonic collection found above. (I will deal with the localised features of the piece in the ongoing analysis of the piece).

There is also a dichotomy between the pitch G# (raised third in the E major areas of the piece) and G natural, found in the ninth bar of the refrain-like second section. G natural is used as an axis of symmetry during the central section of repeated guitar dyads and guitar/bass octaves. The pitches E natural, G natural and G# (Ab) are found in the second collection written above. Tonality and modality are foiled by the Octatonic passages in the piece, in a similar way to Stravinsky's The Firebird Suite where the demonic elements are heightened by Octatonicism.

Red is, essentially, 'on' E rather than 'in' E. The tonality, more of a modality, is offset by the inclusion of tritones, especially A#/Bb. The piece is framed by the ascending Octatonic scales, which are also defined by George Russell in The Lydian Chromatic Concept as 'auxilliary diminished scales', and are responsible for much of what is heard in Red.

Section 1. Introduction:

There are three ascending phrases which launch the ear into the piece. The first of these begins on D# and rises to a high B natural. Guitars 1 & 2 play the octatonic scale in octaves, leaving guitar 3 to provide syncopted, harmonic underlay with the bass.

Guitar 3's function is to not only to be paired with the bass, but to provide the piece with chords and rhythm, supplying an 'edge' to the music. Two bars of 5/8 are followed by a bar of 6/8 before slipping into a bar of 4/4 'on' E.

Phrase one: guitars 1&2 D#-E# (guitar 3 B [major]); guitars 1&2 F#-G# (guitar 3 D [major]); A-B (F [major]); C-D (Ab [major]); E-F#-G-A-B (C [major]); B (E 5ths chord).
Phrase two: B-C# (G [major]; D-E (Bb [major]); F-G (Db [major]); Ab-Bb (Fb [major]); B-C# (G [major]) D-E-F# (Bb [major]); D (D 5ths).
Phrase three, as phrase one except the phrase ends on Bb (tritone from E) over an open E chord in guitar 3.

The underpinning chords present a huge cycle of 3rds.
Phrase one: B-D-F-Ab (outlining a diminished aggregate) C-E (if we include the previous Ab in the last two an augmented aggregate clarifies [Ab-C-E]).
Phrase two: G-Bb-Db-Fb-G-Bb-D.
Phrase three: D (picked up from the previous phrase)-F-Ab-C-E.

Another way might be to regard the introduction as a long dominant prolongation, beginning/prolonging the B (V) and ending on E (I). Also, if the rock element is removed by providing the music with an imaginary 'jazz' approach - by allowing the Octatonic melodic line to 'swing' and transforming the power chords into Major seventh types - we would have an archetypal jazz ending. I have often felt that King Crimson Mk II was a step away from the jazz-influenced Mk I. Sometimes this jazz element can be felt in Mk III, albeit distantly, in the substructures of the songs and pieces.

Section 2:

This is refrain-like in nature, and finds guitars 1 & 2 playing a melodic statement in thirds. Guitar 2 is emphasised: Bb-Ab-Bb-Ab-Bb-Ab-Bb-Ab-Bb-Cb-Bb-Ab-E natural. These pitches are derived from the second of the Octatonic scales of the opening section. Guitar 1 harmonises this a Major 3rd higher: D-C-D-C-D-C-D-C-D-Eb-D-C-G#. Aurally, what develops, is a sound-world which is Augmented in character. (I have spelt the guitar line as flats to retain the Major 3rds, resuming the # notation with the final interval making an E major chord).

Essentially the music at this point of the ritornello/refrain is whole-tone, with passing-notes, underlined by the augmented triads created by the two guitars with the root pitch, E, in the bass and guitar 3. It gives the impression of 'still movement', the rhythmic momentum being decreased by the static harmonic properties. The opening of Liszt's Faust Symphony includes a similar collection of pitches, but in the present context may illustrate Fripp's interest in Debussy's music.

This is repeated. The point to note is that the Bb is a tritone (Lydian 4th) away from the E, and part of the Octatonic collection. The two bar phrase is repeated further, but this time transposed up a tone into F# over two bars. It returns to E X1, then is transposed to G X2, before returning to E X1.

There is a change of metre from 4/4 to 7/8 for the next subsection, with the guitar 2 extending the original melodic motive: Fb-Db-Eb-Db-Fb-Eb. Guitar 1 plays in rhythmic unison, again in thirds, accompanied in the bass (and drums) with rapid Bb semi-quavers. The purpose of this section seems to be to provide the music with further momentum. The music finally comes to ground on E, with the guitar 2 playing oscillating semitones G#-A-G#; G#-D#-E-D#, which is a Fripp musical fingerprint. High resonant triads in a distant guitar 1, E/B/D#, are spaced widely at the top of the texture, providing a wide space between treble and bass in which to place the third guitar open chords and the oscillating semi-tones. This is repeated.

A subsection of B suspensions follows, giving the music a feeling of arrival at the dominant, although Fripp purposely avoids actually stating B major, or B7, chords. The suspensions give a feeling of non-resolution, which is picked-up at the very end of the piece (i.e. the final E major is off-set by the high A#/Bb tritone). These suspended chords are underpinned by the bass guitar pitches: B-D-C. These pitches are related to the bass part of the central section (Section 3), and are re-ordered motivically.

Section 2 is then repeated with transformations: the first eight bars of Section 2 are repeated, except this time the abrupt modulation (really a shift), is omitted leading immediately to a repeat of the 7/8 section. The suspension section then descends in the bass rather ascending using B-A-F#-E. This material includes the descending tone of the 'refrain', as well as outlining a descent from B (V) to E (I). A variant of the 7/8 section follows, thinned and played more softly, the bass playing opposing tritones A (over two bars), and Eb (over two bars), with the guitars playing parallel dyads. This material derives from the following Octatonic collection: A-Bb-C-Db-Eb-E-F#-G. The purpose of this ascent is to prepare the ear for the dramatic central section.

Section 3. The central section:

Bridge passage: the ear is led into the centre of the structure by a bridge passage of three bars of 5/8, with repeated D/Bb dyads over a sustained G in the bass/guitar 3. This connects the previous section 2 to the central section, the kernel of the piece. A chord of G minor is set up in the process, which is a Minor 3rd away from the 'E' centre of Section 2. Minor 3rds have always been an important interval in the piece, and the harmonic shift brings the interval sharply into focus, by presenting it as a structural event rather than as a localised phenomenon.

Texture: the many instances of tritone opposites are mainly nullified during this central section. Here two main musical elements are presented as accompaniment and melody:

a.   repeated dyads guitars 1 & 2;
b.   rhythmically syncopated octave/unison pitches played in the bass and doubled by cello. This is presented in 4/4.

The texture sounds menacing and symphonic, even more so with the omission of the drums, and has something of the flavour of the Russian symphonic tradition: Prokofiev but, more particularly, Shostakovich.

Motives: the bass (cello) part includes the pitches G-E-F/Bb-A-F which illustrates Fripp's methods of re-ordering pitches and using quasi-symmetrical cells. Here a falling Minor 3rd (G-E) is followed by a rising semitone (E-F), followed in the mirroring motive (see above) by a falling semitone and falling Major 3rd. Many of the motives in the central section follow on by using these cells, but not exclusively: sometimes the intervals are expanded into 4ths and 5ths, and the semitones into Major 2nds. In terms of the pitch re-ordering it seems that the composer has taken the bass pitches of the section of suspended chords found in Section 2 (see Part 3 of this analysis), and forged a unity between the music of that section with the music of the central section. For example, the B/D/C heard in the bass part underpinning the B suspended chords of Section 2 are, during the central section, are transformed by transposition and in terms of the direction in which they are played. B/D/C (of Section 2) becomes G/E/F in Section 3. The rising Minor 3rd/falling tone has become a falling Minor 3rd/rising semitone. As in earlier pieces, such as Sailor's Tale (from Islands), much is made from a minimum of musical materials in a closely connected web of motivic and harmonic relationships.

Structure, interval and harmony: there are two distinct halves to the central section. The first begins in G minor and closes with a sustained B minor triad (D, D, F#) with an E root note. The second half repeats some of the first half, but then varies it by the addition of alternative pitches. It also sounds different from the first half, because the guitar dyads are now presented as D/F as opposed to the previous D/Bb, although the tertian harmony (i.e. modulation by pivot pitches) is retained. The use of this technique allows for smooth transitions from one dyad to the next, and is a technique common to most Western classical and jazz musics. There is a particularly striking example of this found in bars 20-21 of the central section where a Db (major) is respelt as a C# (minor). There is also some play between Major and Minor 3rds. This is worked out at a microcosmic level in bar 18 of the section in question, with the pitches G natural and G sharp, as well as being included within the 'container' of the motivic mirrorings. The section comes to rest on a sustained F# / D over a C natural root note. V7d chords, such as this, are found particularly in jazz-rock pieces, but there seems to be no allusion to that genre in Red. I feel that there is a closer affinity with the techniques found in some Eastern European contemporary classical music by using substitute tonal centres (especially Bartok: see Erno Lendvai - The Workshop of Bartok and Kodaly), which suggests Fripp is more than likely conversant with this music, as well as Stravinsky's rhythmic techniques. This is certainly true of Larks' Tongues In Aspic, Parts 1 and 2.

Rhythm: the rhythmic dimension is also closely-knit. During the introduction (Section 1) the opening 5/8 bars (dotted crotchet followed by a crotchet) is transformed and expanded by additive-rhythmic techniques, in the central section, into a dotted crotchet/ dotted crotchet/ crotchet. The 7/8 section is also derived from the opening: there are two instances of dotted quavers followed by semiquavers followed by a quaver and a crotchet. The rhythmic properties of this bar is, in other words, re-shaped and expanded source material. This is a technique particularly favoured by the French composer, Olivier Messiaen. (See Olivier Messiaen: Technique de mon langage musical. Paris, 1944.) It has also been well documented that Messiaen was particularly influenced by the rhythmic dimension of Stravinsky's music.

Section 4. Recapitulation of section 2:

This occurs at the point of the Golden Section. There are 143 bars in Red, and the exact point of Golden Section should be in bar 88. However, the point of recapitulation in Red is at bar 90. For the sake of argument, this must be considered as more or less exact, for a listener can hardly fail to feel it as an important event which includes a certain 'rightness'. Composers such as Schubert, Bartok and Shostakovich have deployed these structural procedures for the positioning of important musical landmarks. Perhaps the finest examples of the technique are to be found in the first movement of Bartok's Fourth String Quartet and Shostakovich's Eighth String Quartet. The material of Section 4 repeats Section 2, with slight modifications. Section 5 goes on to repeat the material of Section 1, this time as a coda, with the Octatonic scales ascending to a high A#/Bb. A# is the leading note to the 'dominant', B, and Bb is the tritonal opposite to the key/modal centre, E.

Structure of the whole: I have already mentioned that the structure is symmetrical - 1. Introduction; 2. Refrain or ritornello; 3. Central; 4. Refrain; 5; Introduction as coda. Composers widely separated in time such as J.S. Bach, Messiaen, Stravinsky, Webern and John Tavener have employed symmetry as a means of conveying important religious symbols, of which the cross and tree seem to take precedence over others. Tavener's works, from the opera Therese onwards, include palindromes for the purpose of conveying icon-like symbols. The first movement of Webern's

Concerto (op.24) displays structural symmetry, as well as harmonic symmetries. This is certainly the case in the Variations for piano (Op. 27). Stravinsky resorts to structural techniques such as palindromes in Canticum Sacrum.

J.S. Bach's Mass in B minor is built in an arch-like shape, and based on a circular key-scheme in the manner of a mandala. The work has two harmonic poles: B minor and D major, the first key referring to human pain, and the second to glory and triumph. G major and G minor stand at the centre of the mandala referring to benediction, with E minor symbolising death. Both E and G bisect the horizontal axis of B and D. The Mass in B minor includes the 'ritornello' principle which I have referred to as 'refrains' in Red. Red also includes the centres of E and G. I am not suggesting that Red is derived from the Mass or, even, that it lies within the Judeo-Christian tradition. However, the symmetrical structure of Red (with G in the centre cutting across the E of the 'refrains') and its key scheme outlining an E minor triad (Section 1: B; 2: E; 3: G; 4: E; 5: B [-E]), whether consciously or unconsciously conceived (as Robert Fripp has said [E-mail to A.G.K. 2nd Feb, 2000]; '...unconscious processes are not...they are a deeper level of the ocean.') - and unlike asymmetrical structures which have implications for the pacing of musical materials - leads one to contemplate alternative meanings.

The psychological interplay within King Crimson at the time of the making of Red may, perhaps, be a governing factor in the making of the music. The accompanying booklet, which includes many of Fripp's Journal entries from the time just prior to the studio recordings of Red, gives a possible insight into this. Symmetrical symbols, especially when concretised in an art-form, sometimes have the effect of creating a Temenos: a sacred 'centre' which mysteriously holds together the tension generated by the opposites in an uncertain situation. Mandalas are a symbol par-excellence of this. The complete structure of Red also illustrates symmetry: 1) Red; 2) Fallen Angel; 3) One More Red Nightmare; 4) Providence; 5) Starless, with One More Red Nightmare referring back to the title piece.

Like In the Court of the Crimson King, Red gives one the feeling that no real resolution is possible. It is tantalising to think that shortly before it was made David Cross had left the group, and shortly after its making the group disbanded. Perhaps the title piece reflects the heat of the tensions through its mandala-like structure, but also goes further in representing the demise of the group? Red, in a sense, conveys the end of a cycle for King Crimson and stands as a book-end to the studio recordings between the five years from 1969-1974. A further reason for connecting ITCOTCK to Red, and to reinforce the notion of a kind of fin-de-siecle, is the guest appearance of Ian McDonald, who left the group in December 1969. This is the first appearance by McDonald on a King Crimson album since that time.

Both ITCOTCK and Red include five pieces. My previous analysis of the former refers to the symbolism of the number 5 in numerological terms: it is the number of fire, strife, competition but, paradoxically, light. A connection could be made with Lucifer who is traditionally thought of as the bringer of light (consciousness) but, at the same time, as the bringer of darkness (unconsciousness).

Red, as a complete work, includes similar paradoxes which continue to prove elusive but, nevertheless, resonate within us. I feel this is the function of 'great' music: not only to give us listening pleasure, but to take us on a multi-dimensional journey touching on the conscious and unconscious parts of our psyches.

Bibliographical Notes

(1) Mojo Magazine. March 2001. Page 60.

(2) New Musical Express. March 17th, 1973.

(3) E-mail from Robert Fripp to the author. 12th March, 2001.

(4) Mojo Magazine. March 2001. Page 60.

(5) E-mail from Robert Fripp to the author. 12th March, 2001.

(6) J.G. Frazer. The Golden Bough. Abridged edition, 1 vol., 1922. New York: Macmillan, 1922.

(7) E-mail from Robert Fripp to the author. 25th March, 2001.

(8) E-mail from Robert Fripp to the author. 12th March, 2001.

(9) Ibid.

(10) Ibid.

(11) Ernö Lendvai. Bela Bartók - an Analysis of his Music. Kahn and Averill. 1971.

(12) E-mail from Robert Fripp to the author. 19th March, 2001.

(13) Ibid.

(14) Ernö Lendvai. Bela Bartók - an Analysis of his Music. Kahn and Averill. 1971.

(15) For a fuller discussion see ibid.

(16) E-mail from Robert Fripp to the author. 20th March, 2001.

(17) Robert Fripp: online Diary. 21st March 2002 www. disciplineglobalmobile.com

18) Jonathan Goldman. Healing Sounds - The Power of Harmonics. Healing Arts Press (www.InnerTraditions.com), 2002. Page 33.

(19) Robin Walker. Form and Meaning in ed. Peter Davison - Reviving the Muse. Essays in Music after Modernism. Claridge Press. 2001. Page 112.

20) David Cross and Andrew Keeling - Cloudsurfing. London Metropolitan University Research Paper. September, 2009. P. 4).

(21) I am grateful to the composer Henry Warwick for this insight.

(22) Gregory Karl. King Crimson's Larks' Tongues In Aspic - A Case of Convergent Evolution in ed. Kevin Holm-Hudson. Progressive Rock Reconsidered. Routledge. 2002. Pages 126-129.

(23) E-mail from Robert Fripp to the author. 12th March, 2001.

(24) Isidore Kaziminsky. Numbers, their Meaning and Magic. Rider and Company. 1985. Pages 17ff.

(25) I am grateful to David Fideler and Michael Schneider for these insights, and to Michael Schneider for the geometrical diagrams of the cover of LTIA. (See www.constructingtheuniverse.com)

(26) I am grateful to Sid Smith for this insight.

(27) E-mail from Robert Fripp to the author 18th March, 2001.

(28) Ibid.

(29) Mojo Magazine. March, 2001. Page 60.

(30) Edward T. Cone. Stravinsky - the Process of a Method in ed. Benjamin Boretz and Edward T. Cone. Perspectives on Schoenberg and Stravinsky. Norton, New York. 1972. Page 156.

(31) E-mail from Robert Fripp to the author. 12th March 2001.

(32) E-mail from Robert Fripp to the author. 5th March 2002.

(33) Ibid.

(34) E-mail from Robert Fripp to to the author. 18th March 2002.

(35) E-mail from David Cross to to the author. 29th May 2009.

Bibliography

(All bibliographical material has been used by permission although one or two sources couldn't be contacted or didn't respond to repeated attempts to make contact. For this we apologise.)

1) Mojo Magazine (2001).
2) New Musical Express (March, 1973).
3) J.G. Frazer - The Golden Bough (Abridged). (N.Y. Macmillan, 1922).
4) Erno Lendvai – Bela Bartok – An Analysis of his Music (Kahn and Averill, 1971).
5) Jonathan Goldman - Healing Sounds - The Power of Harmonics. (Healing Arts Press [www.InnerTraditions.com], 2002).
6) Ed. Peter Davison – Reviving the Muse. Essays in Music after Modernism (Claridge Press, 2001).
7) Ed. Kevin Holm-Hudson – Progressive Rock Reconsidered (Routledge, 2002).
8) Isidore Kaziminsky – Numbers, their Meaning and Magic (Rider and Co. 1985).
9) Ed. Benjamin Boretz and Edward T. Cone – Perspectives on Schoenberg and Stravinsky (Norton, New York, 1972).
10) David Cross and Andrew Keeling. Cloudsurfing. London Metropolitan University Research Paper. September, 2009.

Glossary

Additive/Subtractive rhythms - a feature of Indian music, and explored by the French composer Olivier Messiaen. It is where rhythmic values have extra durations added to them, or subtracted from them.

Aeolian - a white note scale A - A which may be transposed to begin and end on other pitches.

Anacrusis - an upbeat.

Arpeggio (arpeggiation) - a broken chord. Arpeggiations are the playing of the broken chord, with one note following another.

Atonal (Atonality) - that which is termed as being without a fixed key centre. Atonality is associated particularly with the twentieth century Austro-German composers Hauer, Schoenberg, Webern and Berg.

Augmented - a chord which is built from intervals of Major 3rds.

Avant-Garde - a term which has become associated with any

group lying outside an epoch's accepted mode of artistic thinking.

Blues Scale - a modal scale associated with Blues music, having flattened 3rd, 5th and 7th notes.

Cadence - a musical punctuation marking.

Cadenza - a section in a work reserved for the soloist to play alone. Cadenzas were particular popular during the 18th century and are associated mainly with the Concerto.

Counterpoint (Contrapuntal) - where two or more independent musical lines combine so as to create harmony.

Crescendo - becoming louder.

Chromatic - music which employs conjunct (stepwise) motion from white to black notes and so on.

Diminuendo - becoming softer.

Dominant (V) - a chord built on the fifth degree (step) of a key. (In C major the dominant is G major).

Dream Theatre - American progressive metal band formed in 1985.

Embellishment - a musical decoration. Either an ornament or foreground musical material.

Episode (Episodic) - that section of a Baroque Concerto often played by solo instruments as opposed to the whole ensemble. An Episode often connects Ritornello (refrain-like) sections.

False-Relations - similar chords where, although separated in time from each other, one contains a Major 3rd and the other a Minor 3rd.

Gamelan - an Indonesian orchestra comprising metallophones and percussion instruments.

Glissando - sliding up/down a string. The terms glissando and portamento are interchangeable.

Harmony (Harmonic) - two, or more notes, played together vertically as a chord so as to create harmony. The collision of two or more independent musical lines also creates harmony.

Intervals - the distance, between two pitches, is called an interval. (Major 2nd = notes two semitones apart; Minor 3rd = notes three semitones apart; perfect 4th = five semitones apart; Diminished 5th (tritone) = 6 semitones apart; Perfect 5th = seven semitones apart; Minor 6th = eight semitones apart; Major 7th = eleven semitones apart; octave = twelve semitones apart; Minor 13th = twenty semitones apart).

Leading Note - the seventh note in a scale which 'leads' back to the first note (Tonic).

Legato - (to be played) smoothly.

Linear (linearity) - line. Horizontal strands of thematic (melodic) material as opposed to chords which are played vertically.

Mixolydian - a mode usually extending from G-G (white notes) which is also transposable.

Major 2nd - an interval two semitones in distance. (i.e. C - D).

Major 7th chord - a major chord which includes the seventh note found in the scale of the named chord (C major7 would comprise the notes, C, E, G and B).

Minor 3rd - an interval three semitones in distance. (i.e. C - E flat).

Minor 6th - an interval eight semitones in distance. (i.e. C - A flat).

Minor 13th - an interval twenty semitones in distance. (i.e. C - A flat. Also known as a Compound Minor sixth).

Mode (Modality) - a form of scale which originated in ancient

Greece, but probably older. Others were added during the Renaissance. There are several, mainly white note in type: Ionian (C-C); Dorian (D-D); Phrygian (E-E); Lydian (F-F); Mixolydian (G-G); Aeolian (A-A); Locrian (B-B).

Modulate (modulation) - moving to a different key area.

Motive (Motif) - the smallest building blocks of a piece, usually marked by identifiable intervals (melodic or harmonic) or rhythm.

Octaves - notes separated by twelve semitones. (i.e. C - C).

Octatony (Octatonic) - a form of scale with either alternating tones and semitones or semitones with tones.

Ostinato - a repeated note pattern.

Overtone - harmonics.

Passing Notes - unessential notes which pass between two chords without altering the effect of the chords.

Pentatony (Pentatonic) - a form of scale comprising five notes.

Perfect 4th - an interval five semitones in distance. (i.e. C - F)

Perfect 5th - an interval seven semitones in distance. (i.e. C - G).

Pitch-Class - a theoretical term meaning that each note, in a collection of pitches, is designated a number rather than a letter name. (i.e. C=0, C#=1, D=2 etc.)

Polyrhythm (Polyrymthmic) - two, or more, independent rhythmic strands played one over the other.

Power-Chords - powerfully played chords often applied to rock and, particularly, metal which often exclude the third degree of the scale, using notes 1 and 5 together.

Recapitulation - a term often associated with Sonata Form, and defined as a repeat of important musical material.

Resolution - music is said to 'resolve' when it returns to an original key or modal area.

Rhapsody - a piece in an open, fantasy-like form.

Rhythmic Unison - all the performers, in a musical work, play the same rhythmic element together.

Riff - a repeated note pattern. Similar to an ostinato.

Second Inversion - a triad whose pitches have been re-ordered (C major second inversion = G, C, E from the bass upwards).

Sequence - the same melodic strand played higher or lower but retaining an identical shape and sound.

Serial(ism) - a form of music which was innovated by the Austro-German composers Hauer and Schoenberg. Classical serialism is where melodic and harmonic features are governed by a note-row designed pre-compositionally by the composer.

Sonata Form - a term applied to first movements of musical works originating in the Classical period (18th century). Sonata Form denotes a structure where two main themes are heard (Subjects), followed by a Development section (where the thematic material is developed through various means of transformation). The Recapitulation follows where the Subjects are repeated. The piece ends with a Coda.

Stratification - a term coined by the American theorist Edward T. Cone meaning that previous music heard in a work continues to exert an effect in a work even though it may be silent.

Subdominant (IV) - a chord built on the fourth degree (step) of a key. (In C major the subdominant is F major).

Tempo (Tempi) - the speed of a piece.

Texture (Textural) - commonly held to mean the make-up and interaction of sonic elements in a musical work, written or recorded, instrumental or otherwise.

Tonic (I) - the main key of a piece.

Transposition - music which is moved from its original key or mode centre to a new one.

Tremolando - rapidly repeated playing of the same pitch or chord.

Tritone - diminished fifth/augmented fourth. An interval extending six semitones, and standing at an equidistant position in the octave (i.e. C - F sharp). It was known as 'Diabolus in Musica' (the devil in music) in the Medieval church and, as a result, composers were advised not to use the Locrian Mode in their music, which included this interval. (i.e. B - F).

Voice leading - a term used to describe the movement of pitches (part movement) within musical structures.

Glossary - Cited Composers/Musicians

Bartók, Bela (1881-1945) - Hungarian pianist and composer who combined elements of European folk-music with Western art-music.

Britten, Benjamin (1913-1976) - British composer whose opera, Peter Grimes, heralded the resurgence of English post-war opera.

Bryars, Gavin (b. 1943) - British composer and jazz musician associated with the avant-garde in British music during the 1960's and '70's.

Don Caballero - American post-Progressive band influenced as much by Reich as King Crimson.

Emerson, Lake & Palmer - originally described a 'supergroup', comprising Keith Emerson (The Nice), Greg Lake (King Crimson) and Carl Palmer (Atomic Rooster). ELP's album Tarkus (1971) is generally regarded as one of the defining moments of progressive-rock.

Genesis - one of the most important and highly influential of all the bands defined as Progressive with albums such as Nursery Cryme (1971). Band members Peter Gabriel, Phil Collins, Steve Hackett and Mike Rutherford have all gone on to pursue successful solo careers.

Gentle Giant - under-rated yet influential Progressive rock band, whose album Octopus (1972), includes a track, Knots, renowned for its contrapuntal textures.

Hendrix, Jimi (1942-1970) - American guitarist whose extrovert style altered the course of rock music.

Holst, Gustav (1874-1934) - British composer who combined school teaching with composing. His best known work is The Planets.

Mussorgsky, Modest (1839 -1881) - Russian composer who was linked with the group of composers known as The Five.

Nirvana - 1990'2 American Seattle-based Grunge trio made famous through their album Never Mind.

Radiohead - British Indie quintet probably best known for their albums OK Computer (1997) and Kid A (2000).

Rush - Canadian post-progressive trio best known for their albums Farewell to Kings (1977) and (2112).

Schenker, Heinrich (1868 - 1935) - Ukranian born musicologist. Schenker's main intention, throughout his analytical works, was to demonstrate how music ought to be heard.

Skryabin, Alexander (1872-1915) - Russian composer who influenced some of the later, and better known, composers of the twentieth century such as Debussy and Messiaen.

Stravinsky, Igor (1882-1971) - Russian composer whose works are among the most well known in the modern repertoire.

Tavener, Sir John (b. 1944) - British composer whose conversion to the Russian Orthodox Church has influenced many of his more recent works.

The Mahavishnu Orchestra - formed by ex-Miles Davies guitarist John McLaughlin in the early 1970's. The band's best known work is probably The Inner Mountain Flame (1971).

Vaughan Williams, Ralph (1872-1958) - British composer who was influenced by folk music and Tudor church music.

Walker, Robin (b. 1953) - British composer whose works are influenced by the English, often Yorkshire, landscape.

Yes - one of the major bands in the progressive-rock scene of the early 1970's. Their albums Fragile, Close to the Edge and Tales from Topographic Oceans have received both praise and derision at the hands of critics.

Photographs

Photograhs by courtesy of DGM Art Department - with special thanks to Hugh O'Donnel.

Robert Fripp

Robert Fripp

David Cross and Bill Bruford

John Wetton

King Crimson
From left: Jamie Muir, Bill Bruford, Robert Fripp, David Cross and John
Wetton

Bill Bruford and John Wetton

John Wetton

Bill Bruford

David Cross

Jamie Muir

Jamie Muir

Robert Fripp

About The Author

Andrew Keeling's association with King Crimson goes back to 1969 when he first heard In the Court of the Crimson King. He is a composer and musician living in the North of England and has a PhD from the University of Manchester. His orchestrations of Robert Fripp's Soundscapes were performed by the Metropole Orchestra in Amsterdam in 2003 and, as a flautist, he has recently formed an improvisation duo with former King Crimson violinist David Cross.

Also available from Spaceward...

Also by Andrew Keeling

**Musical Guide to In The Court Of The Crimson King
by King Crimson (ISBN 978-0-9562977-0-9)**

and

**Musical Guide to In The Wake Of Poseidon
by King Crimson and McDonald and Giles by McDonald
and Giles (ISBN 978-0-9562977-1-6)**